BEAUTY AND THE BEAST

AND OTHER TALES OF LOVE IN UNEXPECTED PLACES

Amelia Carruthers

ORIGINS OF FAIRY TALES
FROM AROUND THE WORLD

POOK PRESS

Copyright © 2015 Pook Press
An imprint of Read Publishing Ltd.
Home Farm, 44 Evesham Road, Cookhill, Alcester,
Warwickshire, B49 5LJ

Introduced and edited by Amelia Carruthers.
Cover design by Zoë Horn Haywood.
Design by Zoë Horn Haywood and Sam Bigland.

British Library Cataloguing-in-Publication Data. A
catalogue record for this book is available from the
British Library.

Contents

An Introduction to

the Fairy Tale

Fairy Tales are told in almost every society, all over the globe. They have the ability to inspire generations of young and old alike, yet fail to fit neatly into any one mode of storytelling. Today, most people know these narratives through literary works or even film versions, but this is a far cry from the genre's early development. Most of the stories began, and are still propagated through oral traditions, which are still very much alive in certain cultures. Especially in rural, poorer regions, the telling of tales – from village to village, or from elder to younger, preserves culture and custom, whilst still enabling the teller to vary, embellish or adapt the tale as they see fit.

To provide a brief attempt at definition, a fairy tale is a type of short story that typically features 'fantasy' characters, such as dwarves, elves, fairies, giants, gnomes, goblins, mermaids, trolls or witches, and usually magic or enchantments to boot! Fairy tales may be distinguished from other folk narratives such as legends (which generally involve belief in the veracity of the events described) and explicitly moral tales, including fables or those of a religious nature. In cultures where demons and witches are perceived as real, fairy tales may merge into legends, where the narrative is perceived both by teller and hearers as being grounded in historical truth. However unlike legends and epics, they usually do not contain more than superficial references to religion and actual places, people, and events; they take place 'once upon a time' rather than in reality.

The history of the fairy tale is particularly difficult to trace, as most often, it is only the literary forms that are available to the scholar. Still, written evidence indicates that fairy tales have existed for thousands of years, although not perhaps recognized as a genre. Many of today's fairy narratives have evolved from centuries-old stories that have appeared, with variations, in multiple cultures around the world. Two theories of origins have attempted to explain the common elements in fairy tales across continents. One is that a single point of origin generated any given tale, which then spread over the centuries. The other is that such fairy tales stem from common human experience and therefore can appear separately in many different origins. Debates still rage over which interpretation is correct, but as ever, it is likely that a combination of both aspects are involved in the advancements of these folkloric chronicles.

Some folklorists prefer to use the German term *Märchen* or 'wonder tale' to refer to the genre over *fairy tale,* a practice given weight by the definition of Thompson in his 1977 edition of *The Folktale.* He described it as 'a tale of some length involving a succession of motifs or episodes. It moves in an unreal world without definite locality or definite creatures and is filled with the marvellous. In this never-never land, humble heroes kill adversaries, succeed to kingdoms and marry princesses.' The genre was first marked out by writers of the Renaissance, such as Giovanni Francesco Straparola and Giambattista Basile, and stabilized through the works of later collectors such as Charles Perrault and the Brothers Grimm. The oral tradition of the fairy tale came long before the written page however.

Tales were told or enacted dramatically, rather than written down, and handed from generation to generation. Because of this, many fairy tales appear in written literature throughout different cultures, as in *The Golden Ass,* which includes *Cupid and Psyche* (Roman, 100–200 CE), or the *Panchatantra* (India, 3rd century CE). However it is still unknown to what extent these reflect the actual folk tales even of their own time. The 'fairy tale' as a genre became popular among the French nobility of the seventeenth century, and among the tales told were the *Contes* of Charles Perrault (1697), who fixed the forms of 'Sleeping Beauty' and 'Cinderella.' Perrault largely laid the foundations for this new literary variety, with some of the best of his works including 'Puss in Boots', 'Little Red Riding Hood' and 'Bluebeard'.

The first collectors to attempt to preserve not only the plot and characters of the tale, but also the style in which they were told were the Brothers Grimm, who assembled German fairy tales. The Brothers Grimm rejected several tales for their anthology, though told by Germans, because the tales derived from Perrault and they concluded that the stories were thereby *French* and not *German* tales. An oral version of 'Bluebeard' was thus rejected, and the tale of 'Little Briar Rose', clearly related to Perrault's 'The Sleeping Beauty' was included only because Jacob Grimm convinced his brother that the figure of *Brynhildr*, from much earlier Norse mythology, proved that the sleeping princess was authentically German. The Grimm Brothers remain some of the best-known story-tellers of folk tales though, popularising 'Hansel and Gretel', 'Rapunzel', 'Rumplestiltskin' and 'Snow White.'

The work of the Brothers Grimm influenced other collectors, both inspiring them to collect tales and leading them to similarly believe, in a spirit of romantic nationalism, that the fairy tales of a country were particularly representative of it (unfortunately generally ignoring any cross-cultural references). Among those influenced were the Norwegian Peter Christen Asbjørnsen (*Norske Folkeeventyr*, 1842-3), the Russian Alexander Afanasyev (*Narodnye Russkie Skazki,* 1855-63) and the Englishman, Joseph Jacobs (*English Fairy Tales*, 1890). Simultaneously to such developments, writers such as Hans Christian Andersen and George MacDonald continued the tradition of penning original literary fairy tales. Andersen's work sometimes drew on old folktales, but more often deployed fairytale motifs and plots in new stories; for instance in 'The Little Mermaid', 'The Ugly Duckling' and 'The Emperor's New Clothes.'

Fairy tales are still written in the present day, attesting to their enormous popularity and cultural longevity. Aside from their long and diverse literary history, these stories have also been stunningly illustrated by some of the world's best artists – as the reader will be able to see in the following pages. The Golden Age of Illustration (a period customarily defined as lasting from the latter quarter of the nineteenth century until just after the First World War) produced some of the finest examples of this craft, and the masters of the trade are all collected in this volume, alongside the original, inspiring tales. These images form their own story, evolving in conjunction with the literary development of the tales. Consequently, the illustrations are presented in their own narrative sequence, for the reader to appreciate *in and of themselves*. An introduction to the 'Golden Age' can also be found at the end of this book.

THE HISTORY OF
BEAUTY AND THE BEAST

Beauty and the Beast differs from most of the fairy tales in this series, in that, in the form we know it today, it has a reasonably short history. Most fairy tales began as folklore, passed on from generation to generation, until they were eventually written down by collectors such as Giambattista Basile, Charles Perrault or the Brothers Grimm. Unusually, *Beauty and the Beast* does not appear in the anthologies of any of these authors (although the Grimms do have a reasonably similar version in *The Singing Springing Lark*). The tale has gone through many varied and imaginative incarnations, but remaining constant are the themes of envy unrewarded, of learning to love what may at first appear a 'beast' and the benefits which virtue and selflessness will bestow on the individual. *Beauty and the Beast* incorporates several folkloric elements (notably the Aarne-Thompson type of 'The search for the Lost Husband'), and it has a discernable history – first starting with Madame Gabrielle-Suzanne de Villeneuve (1695 - 1755).

Villeneuve was a French author influenced by Madame d'Aulnoy, Charles Perrault and various female intellectuals who gathered in the aristocratic *salons*. Originally published in *La Jeune Américaine, et Les Contes Marins* in 1740, Villeneuve's *La Belle et La Bête* was an original piece of story telling. It was over one-hundred pages long, containing many subplots, and involving a genuinely savage, i.e. 'stupid' Beast, who suffered from not only his change of appearance. The book explored broader themes of romantic love as well as issues surrounding women's marital rights in the mid-eighteenth century. In this period, women had no choice over who they married (it was generally left to their fathers) and had to 'learn to love' the men they were bequeathed to. Villeneuve's story was later changed and shortened by Jeanne-Marie Leprince de Beaumont (1711 - 1780) and published in *Le Magasin des Enfants* (1756). It is this version which readers are most familiar with today, although many elements were omitted from the original tale. Chiefly, in Villeneuve's account (and not in Beaumont's), the back-story of both Belle and the Beast is given. The Beast was a prince who lost his father at a young age, and whose mother had to wage war to defend his kingdom. The queen left him in the care of an evil fairy, who tried to seduce him when he became an adult. When he refused, she transformed him into a beast. Belle's story reveals that she is not really a merchant's daughter but the offspring of a king and a good fairy. The wicked fairy had tried to murder Belle so she could marry her father the king, and Belle was put in the place of a merchant's dead daughter to protect her.

Beaumont significantly pared down the cast of characters and simplified the tale to an almost archetypal simplicity; much loved and repeated. The change from Belle as the offspring of a king and a fairy, to Belle as a simple merchant's daughter is very telling. Beaumont's version, starting with an urban setting is highly unusual in fairy tales, as is the social class of the characters, neither royal nor peasants. Such details reflect the vast social upheavals occurring in France at the time; with the story published just thirty-three years before the French Revolution. This period marked the decline of the powerful monarchy and the church, and the concomitant rise of democracy and nationalism. Popular resentment of the privileges enjoyed by the clergy and aristocracy grew amidst a financial crisis following two expensive wars and years of bad harvests – with demands for change couched in terms of Enlightenment ideals. That the heroine of *La Belle et La Bête* is a simple, working class girl – able to tame the aristocratic beast, spoke directly to the social concerns of the day.

Despite these discernable 'French Enlightenment' beginnings, Bruno Bettelheim has noted in *The Uses of Enchantment* that this story most likely derives from *Cupid and Psyche*, the ancient chronicle from the Latin novel

Metamorphoses, written in the Second Century CE by Apuleius. It concerns the overcoming of obstacles to love between Psyche (meaning 'Soul', or 'Breath of Life') and Cupid (meaning 'Desire') and their ultimate union in marriage. The myth of cupid and psyche is one of the oldest tales to evidence 'the search for the lost husband' trope, and is considered by many scholars to be the first *ever* literary fairy tale. The similarities between this legend and the work of Villeneuve are so striking, it is very likely to be a direct descendent.

The Ancient Roman tale starts with Psyche's banishment (by the jealous Venus) to a mountaintop, in order to be wed to a murderous beast. Sent to destroy her, Cupid falls in love and flies her away to his castle. There, she is directed to never view the face of her husband, who visits and makes love to her in the dark of night. Eventually Psyche succumbs to her curiosity (prompted by her selfish sisters), but accidentally scars her husband with a candle. In attempted atonement, Psyche offers herself as a slave to Venus, and completes a set of impossible tasks. Completing the last task (seeking beauty from the Queen of the Underworld), Psyche opens the 'beauty in a box' and, hoping to gain the approval of her husband, opens the box a little – at once falling into a coma. Overcome with grief, Cupid rescues her. He begs Jupiter that she may become immortal, so that the two could be forever united. Here, instant resemblances can be seen with the character of the beast, banishment to a castle, the deceptive sisters, and true love (mixed with tragedy) ensuring the pair's eternal union.

Even with this tale's ancient beginnings, Apuleius might also have drawn on earlier, oral renditions of the tale from Greek versions; and the Greeks, in turn, may have derived their story from Asian sources since 'Cupid and Psyche' closely reflects the narrative of 'The Woman Who Married a Snake.' This variant first appeared in the Indian *Panchatantra,* a work known to have existed in oral form well before its appearance in print in 500 AD. This helps to explain later variants, where the French beast is replaced by a snake (in the Russian, Chinese and Greek versions), and others – for example in the English variant written by Sidney Oldall Addy, where the 'beast' is a 'Small-tooth dog', a Danish narrative of 'Beauty and the Horse', and the Swiss variant of 'The Bear Prince.' Despite these intriguing discrepancies in the narrative, the best known English version (published by Andrew Lang in 1889) stays with the French roots, representing a complex mix of Villeneuve's and Beaumont's stories.

Lang largely favours Villeneuve's elements of the story (hence its inclusion in this collection, along with Beaumont's account), but also edits out much of the extra dialogue concerning fairies and genealogies. There is another (older) English translation in evidence, that of J. R. Planché (published in 1757), which altered a small but significant part. Instead of asking Belle to marry him each night, the Beast asks: 'May I sleep with you tonight?' The question, whilst obviously more risqué, was not simply erotic. It served to imply control and choice for Belle over her own body and sexuality – something which at that time was not legally hers, nor of any woman handed over as property to her husband. This overt sexuality is repeated in the Russian tale of *The Enchanted Tsarévich,* and the Chinese recitation of *The Fairy Serpent.* In most, the beast is no true beast and never forces his physical desires upon the woman. The Italian narrative of *Zelinda and the Monster* differs in this respect, as the snake persuades the young girl to marry him, only because her father will die if she refuses.

As a testament to this story's ability to inspire and entertain generations of readers, the tale of *Beauty and the Beast* continues to influence popular culture internationally, lending plot elements, allusions and tropes to a wide variety of artistic mediums. It has inspired some of the best fairy tale adaptations in film, from Jean Cocteau's 1946 masterpiece to Disney's *Beauty and the Beast* (1991), a nominee and winner for 'Best Motion Picture' by several Hollywood organizations. With regard to its wide geographical reach, as is evident from even this brief introduction, it has enthused and effected storytelling all over the globe. The story has been translated into almost every language, and very excitingly, is continuing to evolve in the present day. We hope the reader enjoys this collection of some of its best re-tellings.

There lived long, long ago a rich merchant who had three daughters.
Beauty and the Beast and Other Stories, *c.*1920.
Illustrated by John Hassall

CUPID AND PSYCHE

(A Roman / African Tale)

The story of 'Cupid and Psyche' was first told by Lucius Apuleius Madaurensis (*c.* 125 - 180 CE). Apuleius was a Numidian Berber from Madaurus (now M'Daourouch, in present-day Algeria), and studied Platonist philosophy in Athens as well as being an initiate in several cults or *mysteries*. His tale, known formally as the *Metamorphoses* (which has since become known as *The Golden Ass,* as Augustine famously dubbed it) is the only Ancient Roman novel to survive in its entirety. Appearing around 150 CE, the plot revolves around the protagonist's (Lucius's) curiosity, and insatiable desire to see and practice magic – devolving into a series of bawdy and at times ludicrous adventures.

The tale of 'Cupid and Psyche' is presented by Apuleius as an 'old wives tale', recounted by an elderly woman in order to comfort a young girl who had been abducted and held to ransom by a gang of robbers. Its similarities with later versions of 'Beauty and the Beast' are striking; particularly Psyche's curiosity, her subsequent banishment, the role of her deceptive sisters, and true love eventually ensuring the pair's eternal union. This particular version was translated by Thomas Bulfinch (1796 - 1867), an American writer from Massachusetts. He was a well known compiler of mythology, and the text below appears in his *The Age of Fable, or Stories of Gods and Heroes* (1855).

She was known to everyone as Beauty because quite simply, that is what she was.
Beauty and the Beast, 1875.
Illustrated by Eleanor Vere Boyle

A certain king and queen had three daughters. The charms of the two elder were more than common, but the beauty of the youngest was so wonderful that the poverty of language is unable to express its due praise. The fame of her beauty was so great that strangers from neighbouring countries came in crowds to enjoy the sight, and looked on her with amazement, paying her that homage which is due only to Venus herself. In fact Venus found her altars deserted, while men turned their devotion to this young virgin. As she passed along, the people sang her praises, and strewed her way with chaplets and flowers.

This homage to the exaltation of a mortal gave great offense to the real Venus. Shaking her ambrosial locks with indignation, she exclaimed, "Am I then to be eclipsed in my honours by a mortal girl? In vain then did that royal shepherd, whose judgment was approved by Jove himself, give me the palm of beauty over my illustrious rivals, Pallas and Juno. But she shall not so quietly usurp my honours. I will give her cause to repent of so unlawful a beauty."

Thereupon she calls her winged son Cupid, mischievous enough in his own nature, and rouses and provokes him yet more by her complaints. She points out Psyche to him and says, "My dear son, punish that contumacious beauty; give your mother a revenge as sweet as her injuries are great; infuse into the bosom of that haughty girl a passion for some low, mean, unworthy being, so that she may reap a mortification as great as her present exultation and triumph."

Cupid prepared to obey the commands of his mother. There are two fountains in Venus's garden, one of sweet waters, the other of bitter. Cupid filled two amber vases, one from each fountain, and suspending them from the top of his quiver, hastened to the chamber of Psyche, whom he found asleep. He shed a few drops from the bitter fountain over her lips, though the sight of her almost moved him to pity; then touched her side with the point of his arrow. At the touch she awoke, and opened eyes upon Cupid (himself invisible), which so startled him that in his confusion he wounded himself with his own arrow. Heedless of his wound, his whole thought now was to repair the mischief he had done, and he poured the balmy drops of joy over all her silken ringlets.

Psyche, henceforth frowned upon by Venus, derived no benefit from all her charms. True, all eyes were cast eagerly upon her, and every mouth spoke her praises; but neither king, royal youth, nor plebeian presented himself to demand her in marriage. Her two elder sisters of moderate charms had now long been married to two royal princes; but Psyche, in her lonely apartment, deplored her solitude, sick of that beauty which, while it procured abundance of flattery, had failed to awaken love.

Her parents, afraid that they had unwittingly incurred the anger of the gods, consulted the oracle of Apollo, and received this answer, "The virgin is destined for the bride of no mortal lover. Her future husband awaits her on the top of the mountain. He is a monster whom neither gods nor men can resist."

This dreadful decree of the oracle filled all the people with dismay, and her parents abandoned themselves to grief. But Psyche said, "Why, my dear parents, do you now lament me? You should rather have grieved when the people showered upon me undeserved honours, and with one voice called me a Venus. I now perceive that I am a victim to that name. I submit. Lead me to that rock to which my unhappy fate has destined me."

Accordingly, all things being prepared, the royal maid took her place in the procession, which more resembled a funeral than a nuptial pomp, and with her parents, amid the lamentations of the people, ascended the mountain, on the summit of which they left her alone, and with sorrowful hearts returned home.

The two elder girls were ugly disagreeable things.
My Book of Favourite Fairy Tales, 1921.
Illustrated by Jennie Harbour

While Psyche stood on the ridge of the mountain, panting with fear and with eyes full of tears, the gentle Zephyr raised her from the earth and bore her with an easy motion into a flowery dale. By degrees her mind became composed, and she laid herself down on the grassy bank to sleep.

When she awoke refreshed with sleep, she looked round and beheld near a pleasant grove of tall and stately trees. She entered it, and in the midst discovered a fountain, sending forth clear and crystal waters, and fast by, a magnificent palace whose august front impressed the spectator that it was not the work of mortal hands, but the happy retreat of some god. Drawn by admiration and wonder, she approached the building and ventured to enter.

Every object she met filled her with pleasure and amazement. Golden pillars supported the vaulted roof, and the walls were enriched with carvings and paintings representing beasts of the chase and rural scenes, adapted to delight the eye of the beholder. Proceeding onward, she perceived that besides the apartments of state there were others filled with all manner of treasures, and beautiful and precious productions of nature and art.

While her eyes were thus occupied, a voice addressed her, though she saw no one, uttering these words, "Sovereign lady, all that you see is yours. We whose voices you hear are your servants and shall obey all your commands with our utmost care and diligence. Retire, therefore, to your chamber and repose on your bed of down, and when you see fit, repair to the bath. Supper awaits you in the adjoining alcove when it pleases you to take your seat there."

Psyche gave ear to the admonitions of her vocal attendants, and after repose and the refreshment of the bath, seated herself in the alcove, where a table immediately presented itself, without any visible aid from waiters or servants, and covered with

Look at our little sister.

Old Time Stories, 1921.

Illustrated by W. Heath Robinson

Beauty in her prosperous state.
Beauty and the Beast, 1811.
Illustrator Unknown

the greatest delicacies of food and the most nectareous wines. Her ears too were feasted with music from invisible performers; of whom one sang, another played on the lute, and all closed in the wonderful harmony of a full chorus.

She had not yet seen her destined husband. He came only in the hours of darkness and fled before the dawn of morning, but his accents were full of love, and inspired a like passion in her. She often begged him to stay and let her behold him, but he would not consent. On the contrary he charged her to make no attempt to see him, for it was his pleasure, for the best of reasons, to keep concealed.

"Why should you wish to behold me?" he said. "Have you any doubt of my love? Have you any wish ungratified? If you saw me, perhaps you would fear me, perhaps adore me, but all I ask of you is to love me. I would rather you would love me as an equal than adore me as a god."

This reasoning somewhat quieted Psyche for a time, and while the novelty lasted she felt quite happy. But at length the thought of her parents, left in ignorance of her fate, and of her sisters, precluded from sharing with her the delights of her situation, preyed on her mind and made her begin to feel her palace as but a splendid prison. When her husband came one night, she told him her distress, and at last drew from him an unwilling consent that her sisters should be brought to see her.

So, calling Zephyr, she acquainted him with her husband's commands, and he, promptly obedient, soon brought them across the mountain down to their sister's valley. They embraced her and she returned their caresses.

"Come," said Psyche, "enter with me my house and refresh yourselves with whatever your sister has to offer."

A messenger arrived at the palace and told of a violent storm off the coast of Africa.

Beauty and the Beast, 1875.

Illustrated by Eleanor Vere Boyle

Then taking their hands she led them into her golden palace, and committed them to the care of her numerous train of attendant voices, to refresh them in her baths and at her table, and to show them all her treasures. The view of these celestial delights caused envy to enter their bosoms, at seeing their young sister possessed of such state and splendour, so much exceeding their own.

They asked her numberless questions, among others what sort of a person her husband was. Psyche replied that he was a beautiful youth, who generally spent the daytime in hunting upon the mountains.

The sisters, not satisfied with this reply, soon made her confess that she had never seen him. Then they proceeded to fill her bosom with dark suspicions. "Call to mind," they said, "the Pythian oracle that declared you destined to marry a direful and tremendous monster. The inhabitants of this valley say that your husband is a terrible and monstrous serpent, who nourishes you for a while with dainties that he may by and by devour you. Take our advice. Provide yourself with a lamp and a sharp knife; put them in concealment that your husband may not discover them, and when he is sound asleep, slip out of bed, bring forth your lamp, and see for yourself whether what they say is true or not. If it is, hesitate not to cut off the monster's head, and thereby recover your liberty."

Psyche resisted these persuasions as well as she could, but they did not fail to have their effect on her mind, and when her sisters were gone, their words and her own curiosity were too strong for her to resist. So she prepared her lamp and a sharp knife, and hid them out of sight of her husband. When he had fallen into his first sleep, she silently rose and uncovering her lamp beheld not a hideous monster, but the most beautiful and charming of the gods, with his golden ringlets wandering over his snowy neck and crimson cheek, with two dewy wings on his shoulders, whiter than snow, and with shining feathers like the tender blossoms of spring.

As she leaned the lamp over to have a better view of his face, a drop of burning oil fell on the shoulder of the god. Startled, he opened his eyes and fixed them upon her. Then, without saying a word, he spread his white wings and flew out of the window. Psyche, in vain endeavouring to follow him, fell from the window to the ground.

Cupid, beholding her as she lay in the dust, stopped his flight for an instant and said, "Oh foolish Psyche, is it thus you repay my love? After I disobeyed my mother's commands and made you my wife, will you think me a monster and cut off my head? But go; return to your sisters, whose advice you seem to think preferable to mine. I inflict no other punishment on you than to leave you for ever. Love cannot dwell with suspicion." So saying, he fled away, leaving poor Psyche prostrate on the ground, filling the place with mournful lamentations.

When she had recovered some degree of composure she looked around her, but the palace and gardens had vanished, and she found herself in the open field not far from the city where her sisters dwelt. She repaired thither and told them the whole story of her misfortunes, at which, pretending to grieve, those spiteful creatures inwardly rejoiced.

"For now," said they, "he will perhaps choose one of us." With this idea, without saying a word of her intentions, each of them rose early the next morning and ascended the mountain, and having reached the top, called upon Zephyr to receive her and bear her to his lord; then leaping up, and not being sustained by Zephyr, fell down the precipice and was dashed to pieces.

Psyche meanwhile wandered day and night, without food or repose, in search of her husband. Casting her eyes on a lofty mountain having on its brow a magnificent temple, she sighed and said to herself, "Perhaps my love, my lord, inhabits there," and directed her steps thither.

At first she found it very hard.
Old Time Stories, 1921.
Illustrated by W. Heath Robinson

She had no sooner entered than she saw heaps of corn, some in loose ears and some in sheaves, with mingled ears of barley. Scattered about, lay sickles and rakes, and all the instruments of harvest, without order, as if thrown carelessly out of the weary reapers' hands in the sultry hours of the day.

This unseemly confusion the pious Psyche put an end to, by separating and sorting everything to its proper place and kind, believing that she ought to neglect none of the gods, but endeavour by her piety to engage them all in her behalf. The holy Ceres, whose temple it was, finding her so religiously employed, thus spoke to her, "Oh Psyche, truly worthy of our pity, though I cannot shield you from the frowns of Venus, yet I can teach you how best to allay her displeasure. Go, then, and voluntarily surrender yourself to your lady and sovereign, and try by modesty and submission to win her forgiveness, and perhaps her favour will restore you the husband you have lost."

Psyche obeyed the commands of Ceres and took her way to the temple of Venus, endeavouring to fortify her mind and ruminating on what she should say and how best propitiate the angry goddess, feeling that the issue was doubtful and perhaps fatal.

Venus received her with angry countenance. "Most undutiful and faithless of servants," said she, "do you at last remember that you really have a mistress? Or have you rather come to see your sick husband, yet laid up of the wound given him by his loving wife? You are so ill favoured and disagreeable that the only way you can merit your lover must be by dint of industry and diligence. I will make trial of your housewifery." Then she ordered Psyche to be led to the storehouse of her temple, where was laid up a great quantity of wheat, barley, millet, vetches, beans, and lentils prepared for food for her pigeons, and said, "Take and separate all these grains, putting all of the same kind in a parcel by themselves, and see that you get it done before evening." Then Venus departed and left her to her task.

I should like you to bring me home a rose, a lovely red rose, if you can.

My Book of Favourite Fairy Tales, 1921.

Illustrated by Jennie Harbour

The only thing I wish for is to see you come home safely.
The Blue Fairy Book, 1922.
Illustrated by H. J. Ford

But Psyche, in a perfect consternation at the enormous work, sat stupid and silent, without moving a finger to the inextricable heap.

While she sat despairing, Cupid stirred up the little ant, a native of the fields, to take compassion on her. The leader of the anthill, followed by whole hosts of his six-legged subjects, approached the heap, and with the utmost diligence taking grain by grain, they separated the pile, sorting each kind to its parcel; and when it was all done, they vanished out of sight in a moment.

Venus at the approach of twilight returned from the banquet of the gods, breathing odours and crowned with roses. Seeing the task done, she exclaimed, "This is no work of yours, wicked one, but his, whom to your own and his misfortune you have enticed." So saying, she threw her a piece of black bread for her supper and went away.

Next morning Venus ordered Psyche to be called and said to her, "Behold yonder grove which stretches along the margin of the water. There you will find sheep feeding without a shepherd, with golden-shining fleeces on their backs. Go, fetch me a sample of that precious wool gathered from every one of their fleeces."

Psyche obediently went to the riverside, prepared to do her best to execute the command. But the river god inspired the reeds with harmonious murmurs, which seemed to say, "Oh maiden, severely tried, tempt not the dangerous flood, nor venture among the formidable rams on the other side, for as long as they are under the influence of the rising sun, they burn with a cruel rage to destroy mortals with their sharp horns or rude teeth. But when the noontide sun has driven the cattle to the shade, and the serene spirit of the flood has lulled them to rest, you may then cross in safety, and you will find the woolly gold sticking to the bushes and the trunks of the trees."

Thus the compassionate river god gave Psyche instructions how to accomplish her task, and by observing his directions she soon returned to Venus with her arms full of the golden fleece; but she received not the approbation of her implacable mistress, who said, "I know very well it is by none of your own doings that you have succeeded in this task, and I am not satisfied yet that you have any capacity to make yourself useful. But I have another task for you. Here, take this box and go your way to the infernal shades, and give this box to Proserpine and say, 'My mistress Venus desires you to send her a little of your beauty, for in tending her sick son she has lost some of her own.' Be not too long on your errand, for I must paint myself with it to appear at the circle of the gods and goddesses this evening."

Psyche was now satisfied that her destruction was at hand, being obliged to go with her own feet directly down to Erebus. Wherefore, to make no delay of what was not to be avoided, she goes to the top of a high tower to precipitate herself headlong, thus to descend the shortest way to the shades below. But a voice from the tower said to her, "Why, poor unlucky girl, do you design to put an end to your days in so dreadful a manner? And what cowardice makes you sink under this last danger who have been so miraculously supported in all your former?" Then the voice told her how by a certain cave she might reach the realms of Pluto, and how to avoid all the dangers of the road, to pass by Cerberus, the three-headed dog, and prevail on Charon, the ferryman, to take her across the black river and bring her back again. But the voice added, "When Proserpine has given you the box filled with her beauty, of all things this is chiefly to be observed by you, that you never once open or look into the box nor allow your curiosity to pry into the treasure of the beauty of the goddesses."

Psyche, encouraged by this advice, obeyed it in all things, and taking heed to her ways travelled safely to the kingdom of Pluto. She was admitted to the palace of Proserpine, and without accepting the delicate seat or delicious banquet that was offered her, but contented with coarse bread for her food, she delivered her

The merchant set off on a journey which he hoped would restore his fortunes.

Beauty and the Beast, 1875.

Illustrated by Eleanor Vere Boyle

Beauty and the Beast.
Four and Twenty Fairy Tales, 1858.
Illustrated by Edward Corbould

message from Venus. Presently the box was returned to her, shut and filled with the precious commodity. Then she returned the way she came, and glad was she to come out once more into the light of day.

But having got so far successfully through her dangerous task a longing desire seized her to examine the contents of the box. "What," said she, "shall I, the carrier of this divine beauty, not take the least bit to put on my cheeks to appear to more advantage in the eyes of my beloved husband!" So she carefully opened the box, but found nothing there of any beauty at all, but an infernal and truly Stygian sleep, which being thus set free from its prison, took possession of her, and she fell down in the midst of the road, a sleepy corpse without sense or motion.

But Cupid, being now recovered from his wound, and not able longer to bear the absence of his beloved Psyche, slipping through the smallest crack of the window of his chamber which happened to be left open, flew to the spot where Psyche lay, and gathering up the sleep from her body closed it again in the box, and waked Psyche with a light touch of one of his arrows. "Again," said he, "have you almost perished by the same curiosity. But now perform exactly the task imposed on you by my mother, and I will take care of the rest."

Then Cupid, as swift as lightning penetrating the heights of heaven, presented himself before Jupiter with his supplication. Jupiter lent a favouring ear, and pleaded the cause of the lovers so earnestly with Venus that he won her consent. On this he sent Mercury to bring Psyche up to the heavenly assembly, and when she arrived, handing her a cup of ambrosia, he said, "Drink this, Psyche, and be immortal; nor shall Cupid ever break away from the knot in which he is tied, but these nuptials shall be perpetual."

Thus Psyche became at last united to Cupid, and in due time they had a daughter born to them whose name was Pleasure.

It was snowing horribly.
Old Time Stories, 1921.
Illustrated by W. Heath Robinson

La Belle et La Bête

(A French Tale)

This story was first published by Jeanne-Marie Leprince de Beaumont in 1756, as 'a tale for the entertainment of juvenile readers.' Beaumont (1711 - 1780) wrote the tale whilst working as a governess in London, after which she enjoyed a successful publishing career. It first appeared under the title of 'La Belle et La Bête' in *Magasin des Enfants, ou Dialogues entre une Sage Gouvernante et Plusieurs de ses Élèves* (The Young Misses Magazine, Containing Dialogues between a Wise Governess and Several of Her Students). Beaumont was responding to an earlier, much lengthier version of the story though – that of Gabrielle-Suzanne Barbot de Villeneuve (1695 - 1755), which first appeared in 1740.

Although similar in the overall plot, Beaumont changed many aspects of Villeneuve's original, omitting various details to fit a younger audience and giving a more didactic message about good manners and behaviour. Most obvious is the lack of any back-story for Belle and the Beast, as well as the paring down of the cast of characters. Particularly remarkable is the urban opening, highly unusual in fairy tales. The social class of the characters is also worthy of note; neither royal nor peasants, they occupy a unique space in folkloric storytelling. This ability of Beaumont, to adapt and re-appropriate pre-existing narratives, has ensured the tale's continued popularity – with her version still the best-loved variant to this day.

He had been fasting for more than twenty-four hours, and lost no time in falling to.
The Sleeping Beauty and Other Fairy Tales From the Old French, 1910.
Illustrated by Edmund Dulac

There was once a very rich merchant, who had six children, three sons, and three daughters; being a man of sense, he spared no cost for their education, but gave them all kinds of masters. His daughters were extremely handsome, especially the youngest. When she was little everybody admired her, and called her "The little Beauty;" so that, as she grew up, she still went by the name of Beauty, which made her sisters very jealous.

The youngest, as she was handsomer, was also better than her sisters. The two eldest had a great deal of pride, because they were rich. They gave themselves ridiculous airs, and would not visit other merchants' daughters, nor keep company with any but persons of quality. They went out every day to parties of pleasure, balls, plays, concerts, and so forth, and they laughed at their youngest sister, because she spent the greatest part of her time in reading good books.

As it was known that they were great fortunes, several eminent merchants made their addresses to them; but the two eldest said, they would never marry, unless they could meet with a duke, or an earl at least. Beauty very civilly thanked them that courted her, and told them she was too young yet to marry, but chose to stay with her father a few years longer.

All at once the merchant lost his whole fortune, excepting a small country house at a great distance from town, and told his children with tears in his eyes, they must go there and work for their living. The two eldest answered, that they would not leave the town, for they had several lovers, who they were sure would be glad to have them, though they had no fortune; but the good ladies were mistaken, for their lovers slighted and forsook them in their poverty. As they were not beloved on account of their pride, everybody said; they do not deserve to be pitied, we are very glad to see their pride humbled, let them go and give themselves quality airs in milking the cows and minding their dairy. But, added they, we are extremely concerned for Beauty, she was such a charming, sweet-tempered creature, spoke so kindly to poor people, and was of such an affable, obliging behaviour. Nay, several gentlemen would have married her, though they knew she had not a penny; but she told them she could not think of leaving her poor father in his misfortunes, but was determined to go along with him into the country to comfort and attend him. Poor Beauty at first was sadly grieved at the loss of her fortune; "but," said she to herself, "were I to cry ever so much, that would not make things better, I must try to make myself happy without a fortune."

When they came to their country house, the merchant and his three sons applied themselves to husbandry and tillage; and Beauty rose at four in the morning, and made haste to have the house clean, and dinner ready for the family. In the beginning she found it very difficult, for she had not been used to work as a servant, but in less than two months she grew stronger and healthier than ever. After she had done her work, she read, played on the harpsichord, or else sung whilst she spun.

On the contrary, her two sisters did not know how to spend their time; they got up at ten, and did nothing but saunter about the whole day, lamenting the loss of their fine clothes and acquaintance. "Do but see our youngest sister," said they, one to the other, "what a poor, stupid, mean-spirited creature she is, to be contented with such an unhappy dismal situation."

The good merchant was of quite a different opinion; he knew very well that Beauty outshone her sisters, in her person as well as her mind, and admired her humility and industry, but above all her humility and patience; for her sisters not only left her all the work of the house to do, but insulted her every moment.

The family had lived about a year in this retirement, when the merchant received a letter with an account that a vessel, on board of which he had effects,

Saw a beast coming towards him which was so hideous that he came near to fainting.

Old Time Stories, 1921.

Illustrated by W. Heath Robinson

was safely arrived. This news had liked to have turned the heads of the two eldest daughters, who immediately flattered themselves with the hopes of returning to town, for they were quite weary of a country life; and when they saw their father ready to set out, they begged of him to buy them new gowns, headdresses, ribbons, and all manner of trifles; but Beauty asked for nothing for she thought to herself, that all the money her father was going to receive, would scarce be sufficient to purchase everything her sisters wanted.

"What will you have, Beauty?" said her father.

"Since you have the goodness to think of me," answered she, "be so kind to bring me a rose, for as none grows hereabouts, they are a kind of rarity." Not that Beauty cared for a rose, but she asked for something, lest she should seem by her example to condemn her sisters' conduct, who would have said she did it only to look particular.

The good man went on his journey, but when he came there, they went to law with him about the merchandise, and after a great deal of trouble and pains to no purpose, he came back as poor as before.

He was within thirty miles of his own house, thinking on the pleasure he should have in seeing his children again, when going through a large forest he lost himself. It rained and snowed terribly; besides, the wind was so high, that it threw him twice off his horse, and night coming on, he began to apprehend being either starved to death with cold and hunger, or else devoured by the wolves, whom he heard howling all round him, when, on a sudden, looking through a long walk of trees, he saw a light at some distance, and going on a little farther perceived it came from a palace illuminated from top to bottom. The merchant returned God thanks for this happy discovery, and hastened to the place, but was greatly surprised at not meeting with any one in the outer courts. His horse followed him, and seeing a large stable open, went in, and

Directly after he had plucked the rose the merchant saw a monster with a beast's head but of the shape of a man, who stood glaring at him in a threatening manner.

Fairy Tales, 1915.

Illustrated by Margaret Tarrant

He had no sooner taken it than he saw a hideous beast.

Beauty and the Beast, 1873.

Illustrated by Walter Crane

finding both hay and oats, the poor beast, who was almost famished, fell to eating very heartily; the merchant tied him up to the manger, and walking towards the house, where he saw no one, but entering into a large hall, he found a good fire, and a table plentifully set out with but one cover laid. As he was wet quite through with the rain and snow, he drew near the fire to dry himself. "I hope," said he, "the master of the house, or his servants will excuse the liberty I take; I suppose it will not be long before some of them appear."

He waited a considerable time, until it struck eleven, and still nobody came. At last he was so hungry that he could stay no longer, but took a chicken, and ate it in two mouthfuls, trembling all the while. After this he drank a few glasses of wine, and growing more courageous he went out of the hall, and crossed through several grand apartments with magnificent furniture, until he came into a chamber, which had an exceeding good bed in it, and as he was very much fatigued, and it was past midnight, he concluded it was best to shut the door, and go to bed.

It was ten the next morning before the merchant waked, and as he was going to rise he was astonished to see a good suit of clothes in the room of his own, which were quite spoiled; certainly, said he, this palace belongs to some kind fairy, who has seen and pitied my distress. He looked through a window, but instead of snow saw the most delightful arbors, interwoven with the beautifullest flowers that were ever beheld. He then returned to the great hall, where he had supped the night before, and found some chocolate ready made on a little table. "Thank you, good Madam Fairy," said he aloud, "for being so careful, as to provide me a breakfast; I am extremely obliged to you for all your favours."

The good man drank his chocolate, and then went to look for his horse, but passing through an arbor of roses he remembered Beauty's request to him, and gathered a branch on which were several; immediately he heard a great noise, and saw such a frightful Beast coming towards him, that he was ready to faint away.

"You are very ungrateful," said the Beast to him, in a terrible voice; "I have saved your life by receiving you into my castle, and, in return, you steal my roses, which I value beyond any thing in the universe, but you shall die for it; I give you but a quarter of an hour to prepare yourself, and say your prayers."

The merchant fell on his knees, and lifted up both his hands, "My lord," said he, "I beseech you to forgive me, indeed I had no intention to offend in gathering a rose for one of my daughters, who desired me to bring her one."

"My name is not My Lord," replied the monster, "but Beast; I don't love compliments, not I. I like people to speak as they think; and so do not imagine, I am to be moved by any of your flattering speeches. But you say you have got daughters. I will forgive you, on condition that one of them come willingly, and suffer for you. Let me have no words, but go about your business, and swear that if your daughter refuse to die in your stead, you will return within three months."

The merchant had no mind to sacrifice his daughters to the ugly monster, but he thought, in obtaining this respite, he should have the satisfaction of seeing them once more, so he promised, upon oath, he would return, and the Beast told him he might set out when he pleased, "but," added he, "you shall not depart empty handed; go back to the room where you lay, and you will see a great empty chest; fill it with whatever you like best, and I will send it to your home," and at the same time Beast withdrew.

"Well," said the good man to himself, "if I must die, I shall have the comfort, at least, of leaving something to my poor children." He returned to the bedchamber, and finding a great quantity of broad pieces of gold, he filled

The merchant and the beast.
Beauty and the Beast, 1885.
Published by Peter G. Thomson

Turning round he saw a frightful beast.
The Blue Fairy Book, 1922.
Illustrated by H. J. Ford

the great chest the Beast had mentioned, locked it, and afterwards took his horse out of the stable, leaving the palace with as much grief as he had entered it with joy. The horse, of his own accord, took one of the roads of the forest, and in a few hours the good man was at home.

His children came round him, but instead of receiving their embraces with pleasure, he looked on them, and holding up the branch he had in his hands, he burst into tears. "Here, Beauty," said he, "take these roses, but little do you think how dear they are like to cost your unhappy father," and then related his fatal adventure. Immediately the two eldest set up lamentable outcries, and said all manner of ill-natured things to Beauty, who did not cry at all.

"Do but see the pride of that little wretch," said they; "she would not ask for fine clothes, as we did; but no truly, Miss wanted to distinguish herself, so now she will be the death of our poor father, and yet she does not so much as shed a tear."

"Why should I," answered Beauty, "it would be very needless, for my father shall not suffer upon my account, since the monster will accept of one of his daughters, I will deliver myself up to all his fury, and I am very happy in thinking that my death will save my father's life, and be a proof of my tender love for him."

"No, sister," said her three brothers, "that shall not be, we will go find the monster, and either kill him, or perish in the attempt."

"Do not imagine any such thing, my sons," said the merchant, "Beast's power is so great, that I have no hopes of your overcoming him. I am charmed with Beauty's kind and generous offer, but I cannot yield to it. I am old, and have not long to live, so can only loose a few years, which I regret for your sakes alone, my dear children."

"Indeed father," said Beauty, "you shall not go to the palace without me, you cannot hinder me from following you." It was to no purpose all they could say. Beauty still insisted on setting out for the fine palace, and her sisters were delighted at it, for her virtue and amiable qualities made them envious and jealous.

The merchant was so afflicted at the thoughts of losing his daughter, that he had quite forgot the chest full of gold, but at night when he retired to rest, no sooner had he shut his chamber door, than, to his great astonishment, he found it by his bedside; he was determined, however, not to tell his children, that he was grown rich, because they would have wanted to return to town, and he was resolved not to leave the country; but he trusted Beauty with the secret, who informed him, that two gentlemen came in his absence, and courted her sisters; she begged her father to consent to their marriage, and give them fortunes, for she was so good, that she loved them and forgave heartily all their ill usage. These wicked creatures rubbed their eyes with an onion to force some tears when they parted with their sister, but her brothers were really concerned. Beauty was the only one who did not shed tears at parting, because she would not increase their uneasiness.

The horse took the direct road to the palace, and towards evening they perceived it illuminated as at first. The horse went of himself into the stable, and the good man and his daughter came into the great hall, where they found a table splendidly served up, and two covers. The merchant had no heart to eat, but Beauty, endeavouring to appear cheerful, sat down to table, and helped him. "Afterwards," thought she to herself, "Beast surely has a mind to fatten me before he eats me, since he provides such plentiful entertainment." When they had supped they heard a great noise, and the merchant, all in tears, bid his poor child, farewell, for he thought Beast was coming. Beauty was sadly terrified at his horrid form, but she took courage as well as she could, and the monster having asked her if she came willingly; "ye -- e -- es," said she, trembling.

He heard a noise, and saw coming towards him a beast, so frightful to look at that he was ready to faint with fear.

The Arthur Rackham Fairy Book, 1933.

Illustrated by Arthur Rackham

The rose gather'd.

Beauty and the Beast, 1811.

Illustrator Unknown

The beast responded, "You are very good, and I am greatly obliged to you; honest man, go your ways tomorrow morning, but never think of coming here again."

"Farewell Beauty, farewell Beast," answered he, and immediately the monster withdrew. "Oh, daughter," said the merchant, embracing Beauty, "I am almost frightened to death, believe me, you had better go back, and let me stay here."

"No, father," said Beauty, in a resolute tone, "you shall set out tomorrow morning, and leave me to the care and protection of providence." They went to bed, and thought they should not close their eyes all night; but scarce were they laid down, than they fell fast asleep, and Beauty dreamed, a fine lady came, and said to her, "I am content, Beauty, with your good will, this good action of yours in giving up your own life to save your father's shall not go unrewarded." Beauty waked, and told her father her dream, and though it helped to comfort him a little, yet he could not help crying bitterly, when he took leave of his dear child.

As soon as he was gone, Beauty sat down in the great hall, and fell a crying likewise; but as she was mistress of a great deal of resolution, she recommended herself to God, and resolved not to be uneasy the little time she had to live; for she firmly believed Beast would eat her up that night.

However, she thought she might as well walk about until then, and view this fine castle, which she could not help admiring; it was a delightful pleasant place, and she was extremely surprised at seeing a door, over which was written, "Beauty's Apartment." She opened it hastily, and was quite dazzled with the magnificence that reigned throughout; but what chiefly took up her attention, was a large library, a harpsichord, and several music books. "Well," said she to herself, "I see they will not let my time hang heavy upon my hands for want of amusement." Then she reflected, "Were I but to stay here a day, there would not have been all these preparations." This consideration inspired her with fresh courage; and opening the library she took a book, and read these words, in letters of gold:

> Welcome Beauty, banish fear,
> You are queen and mistress here.
> Speak your wishes, speak your will,
> Swift obedience meets them still.

"Alas," said she, with a sigh, "there is nothing I desire so much as to see my poor father, and know what he is doing." She had no sooner said this, when casting her eyes on a great looking glass, to her great amazement, she saw her own home, where her father arrived with a very dejected countenance. Her sisters went to meet him, and notwithstanding their endeavours to appear sorrowful, their joy, felt for having got rid of their sister, was visible in every feature. A moment after, everything disappeared, and Beauty's apprehensions at this proof of Beast's complaisance.

At noon she found dinner ready, and while at table, was entertained with an excellent concert of music, though without seeing anybody. But at night, as she was going to sit down to supper, she heard the noise Beast made, and could not help being sadly terrified. "Beauty," said the monster, "will you give me leave to see you sup?"

"That is as you please," answered Beauty trembling.

"No," replied the Beast, "you alone are mistress here; you need only bid me gone, if my presence is troublesome, and I will immediately withdraw. But, tell me, do not you think me very ugly?"

He heard a terrible roar and there, before him, loomed a hideous beast.

Beauty and the Beast, 1875.

Illustrated by Eleanor Vere Boyle

Fill it with whatever you like best, and I will get it conveyed to your own house.

The Big Book of Fairy Tales, 1911.

Illustrated by Charles Robinson

"That is true," said Beauty, "for I cannot tell a lie, but I believe you are very good natured."

"So I am," said the monster, "but then, besides my ugliness, I have no sense; I know very well, that I am a poor, silly, stupid creature."

"'Tis no sign of folly to think so," replied Beauty, "for never did fool know this, or had so humble a conceit of his own understanding."

"Eat then, Beauty," said the monster, "and endeavour to amuse yourself in your palace, for everything here is yours, and I should be very uneasy, if you were not happy."

"You are very obliging," answered Beauty, "I own I am pleased with your kindness, and when I consider that, your deformity scarce appears."

"Yes, yes," said the Beast, "my heart is good, but still I am a monster."

"Among mankind," says Beauty, "there are many that deserve that name more than you, and I prefer you, just as you are, to those, who, under a human form, hide a treacherous, corrupt, and ungrateful heart."

"If I had sense enough," replied the Beast, "I would make a fine compliment to thank you, but I am so dull, that I can only say, I am greatly obliged to you."

Beauty ate a hearty supper, and had almost conquered her dread of the monster; but she had like to have fainted away, when he said to her, "Beauty, will you be my wife?"

She was some time before she dared answer, for she was afraid of making him angry, if she refused. At last, however, she said trembling, "no Beast."

Immediately the poor monster went to sigh, and hissed so frightfully, that the whole palace echoed. But Beauty soon recovered her fright, for Beast having said, in a mournful voice, "then farewell, Beauty," left the room; and only turned back, now and then, to look at her as he went out.

When Beauty was alone, she felt a great deal of compassion for poor Beast. "Alas," said she, "'tis thousand pities, anything so good natured should be so ugly."

Beauty spent three months very contentedly in the palace. Every evening Beast paid her a visit, and talked to her, during supper, very rationally, with plain good common sense, but never with what the world calls wit; and Beauty daily discovered some valuable qualifications in the monster, and seeing him often had so accustomed her to his deformity, that, far from dreading the time of his visit, she would often look on her watch to see when it would be nine, for the Beast never missed coming at that hour. There was but one thing that gave Beauty any concern, which was, that every night, before she went to bed, the monster always asked her, if she would be his wife. One day she said to him, "Beast, you make me very uneasy, I wish I could consent to marry you, but I am too sincere to make you believe that will ever happen; I shall always esteem you as a friend, endeavour to be satisfied with this."

"I must," said the Beast, "for, alas! I know too well my own misfortune, but then I love you with the tenderest affection. However, I ought to think myself happy, that you will stay here; promise me never to leave me."

Beauty blushed at these words; she had seen in her glass, that her father had pined himself sick for the loss of her, and she longed to see him again. "I could," answered she, "indeed, promise never to leave you entirely, but I have so great a desire to see my father, that I shall fret to death, if you refuse me that satisfaction."

Her father was just arriving.
Tales of Passed Times, 1900.
Illustrated by Charles Robinson

Giving Beauty the rose, he told her all.
Beauty and the Beast, 1873.
Illustrated by Walter Crane

"I had rather die myself," said the monster, "than give you the least uneasiness. I will send you to your father, you shall remain with him, and poor Beast will die with grief."

"No," said Beauty, weeping, "I love you too well to be the cause of your death. I give you my promise to return in a week. You have shown me that my sisters are married, and my brothers gone to the army; only let me stay a week with my father, as he is alone."

"You shall be there tomorrow morning," said the Beast, "but remember your promise. You need only lay your ring on a table before you go to bed, when you have a mind to come back. Farewell Beauty." Beast sighed, as usual, bidding her good night, and Beauty went to bed very sad at seeing him so afflicted. When she waked the next morning, she found herself at her father's, and having rung a little bell, that was by her bedside, she saw the maid come, who, the moment she saw her, gave a loud shriek, at which the good man ran up stairs, and thought he should have died with joy to see his dear daughter again. He held her fast locked in his arms above a quarter of an hour. As soon as the first transports were over, Beauty began to think of rising, and was afraid she had no clothes to put on; but the maid told her, that she had just found, in the next room, a large trunk full of gowns, covered with gold and diamonds. Beauty thanked good Beast for his kind care, and taking one of the plainest of them, she intended to make a present of the others to her sisters. She scarce had said so when the trunk disappeared. Her father told her, that Beast insisted on her keeping them herself, and immediately both gowns and trunk came back again.

Beauty dressed herself, and in the meantime they sent to her sisters who hastened thither with their husbands. They were both of them very unhappy. The eldest had married a gentleman, extremely handsome indeed, but so fond of his own person, that he was full of nothing but his own dear self, and neglected his wife. The second had married a man of wit, but he only made use of it to plague and torment everybody, and his wife most of all. Beauty's sisters sickened with envy, when they saw her dressed like a princess, and more beautiful than ever, nor could all her obliging affectionate behaviour stifle their jealousy, which was ready to burst when she told them how happy she was. They went down into the garden to vent it in tears; and said one to the other, in what way is this little creature better than us, that she should be so much happier? "Sister," said the oldest, "a thought just strikes my mind; let us endeavour to detain her above a week, and perhaps the silly monster will be so enraged at her for breaking her word, that he will devour her."

"Right, sister," answered the other, "therefore we must show her as much kindness as possible." After they had taken this resolution, they went up, and behaved so affectionately to their sister, that poor Beauty wept for joy. When the week was expired, they cried and tore their hair, and seemed so sorry to part with her, that she promised to stay a week longer.

In the meantime, Beauty could not help reflecting on herself, for the uneasiness she was likely to cause poor Beast, whom she sincerely loved, and really longed to see again. The tenth night she spent at her father's, she dreamed she was in the palace garden, and that she saw Beast extended on the grass plat, who seemed just expiring, and, in a dying voice, reproached her with her ingratitude. Beauty started out of her sleep, and bursting into tears. "Am I not very wicked," said she, "to act so unkindly to Beast, that has studied so much, to please me in everything? Is it his fault if he is so ugly, and has so little sense? He is kind and good, and that is sufficient. Why did I refuse to marry him? I should be happier with the monster than my sisters are with their husbands; it is neither wit, nor a fine person, in a husband, that makes a woman happy, but virtue, sweetness of temper, and complaisance, and Beast has all these valuable qualifications. It is true, I do not feel the tenderness of affection for him, but I find I have the highest gratitude, esteem, and friendship; I will not make him

Beauty takes her father's place.
Beauty and the Beast, 1885.
Published by Peter G. Thomson

miserable, were I to be so ungrateful I should never forgive myself." Beauty having said this, rose, put her ring on the table, and then laid down again; scarce was she in bed before she fell asleep, and when she waked the next morning, she was overjoyed to find herself in the Beast's palace.

She put on one of her richest suits to please him, and waited for evening with the utmost impatience, at last the wished-for hour came, the clock struck nine, yet no Beast appeared. Beauty then feared she had been the cause of his death; she ran crying and wringing her hands all about the palace, like one in despair; after having sought for him everywhere, she recollected her dream, and flew to the canal in the garden, where she dreamed she saw him. There she found poor Beast stretched out, quite senseless, and, as she imagined, dead. She threw herself upon him without any dread, and finding his heart beat still, she fetched some water from the canal, and poured it on his head. Beast opened his eyes, and said to Beauty, "You forgot your promise, and I was so afflicted for having lost you, that I resolved to starve myself, but since I have the happiness of seeing you once more, I die satisfied."

"No, dear Beast," said Beauty, "you must not die. Live to be my husband; from this moment I give you my hand, and swear to be none but yours. Alas! I thought I had only a friendship for you, but the grief I now feel convinces me, that I cannot live without you." Beauty scarce had pronounced these words, when she saw the palace sparkle with light; and fireworks, instruments of music, everything seemed to give notice of some great event. But nothing could fix her attention; she turned to her dear Beast, for whom she trembled with fear; but how great was her surprise! Beast was disappeared, and she saw, at her feet, one of the loveliest princes that eye ever beheld; who returned her thanks for having put an end to the charm, under which he had so long resembled a Beast. Though this prince was worthy of all her attention, she could not forbear asking where Beast was.

Soon they caught sight of the castle in the distance.
The Sleeping Beauty and Other Fairy Tales From the Old French, 1910.
Illustrated by Edmund Dulac

"You see him at your feet, said the prince. A wicked fairy had condemned me to remain under that shape until a beautiful virgin should consent to marry me. The fairy likewise enjoined me to conceal my understanding. There was only you in the world generous enough to be won by the goodness of my temper, and in offering you my crown I can't discharge the obligations I have to you."

Beauty, agreeably surprised, gave the charming prince her hand to rise; they went together into the castle, and Beauty was overjoyed to find, in the great hall, her father and his whole family, whom the beautiful lady, that appeared to her in her dream, had conveyed thither.

"Beauty," said this lady, "come and receive the reward of your judicious choice; you have preferred virtue before either wit or beauty, and deserve to find a person in whom all these qualifications are united. You are going to be a great queen. I hope the throne will not lessen your virtue, or make you forget yourself. As to you, ladies," said the fairy to Beauty's two sisters, "I know your hearts, and all the malice they contain. Become two statues, but, under this transformation, still retain your reason. You shall stand before your sister's palace gate, and be it your punishment to behold her happiness; and it will not be in your power to return to your former state, until you own your faults, but I am very much afraid that you will always remain statues. Pride, anger, gluttony, and idleness are sometimes conquered, but the conversion of a malicious and envious mind is a kind of miracle."

Immediately the fairy gave a stroke with her wand, and in a moment all that were in the hall were transported into the prince's dominions. His subjects received him with joy. He married Beauty, and lived with her many years, and their happiness -- as it was founded on virtue -- was complete.

They reached the palace in a few hours.
The Big Book of Fairy Tales, 1911.
Illustrated by Charles Robinson

When she came to the gate in the wall she knocked upon it three times.
My Book of Favourite Fairy Tales, 1921.

Illustrated by Jennie Harbour

ZELINDA AND THE MONSTER

(An Italian Tale)

'Zelinda and the Monster' was recorded in Thomas Frederick Crane's *Italian Popular Tales*, published in 1885. Crane (1844 - 1927) was an American folklorist, academic and lawyer – one of the founders of the *Journal of American Folklore*, a pioneering peer-reviewed academic journal which aimed to encourage research into, and dissemination of, folkloric traditions.

'Zelinda and the Monster' differs from the classic Beaumont version, in that the father is depicted as a poor man, with only three daughters instead of six children. The 'Beast' is no ordinary beast in this version either, but a fire breathing dragon who requests the presence of his daughter. In a similar manner to Villeneuve's early tale, the dragon 'caresses' beauty instead of just asking her to marry him, but, like Belle – the young girl always turns him down. The twist in the tale comes with the Dragon's ability to change Zelinda's mind, and the reader never learns whether she is reunited with her family. Similarly to the ancient legend of 'Cupid and Psyche', the jealous sisters are featured – typically resentful of their younger sibling's happiness.

>———→

There was once a poor man who had three daughters; and as the youngest was the fairest and most civil, and had the best disposition, her other two sisters envied her with a deadly envy, although her father, on the contrary, loved her dearly. It happened that in a neighbouring town, in the month of January, there was a great fair, and that poor man was obliged to go there to lay in the provisions necessary for the support of his family; and before departing he asked his three daughters if they would like some small presents in proportion, you understand, to his means. Rosina wished a dress, Marietta asked him for a shawl, but Zelinda was satisfied with a handsome rose.

The poor man set out on his journey early the next day, and when he arrived at the fair quickly bought what he needed, and afterward easily found Rosina's dress and Marietta's shawl; but at that season he could not find a rose for his Zelinda, although he took great pains in looking everywhere for one. However, anxious to please his dear Zelinda, he took the first road he came to, and after journeying a while arrived at a handsome garden enclosed by high walls; but as the gate was partly open he entered softly. He found the garden filled with every kind of flowers and plants, and in a corner was a tall rosebush full of beautiful rosebuds. Wherever he looked no living soul appeared from whom he might ask a rose as a gift or for money, so the poor man, without thinking, stretched out his hand, and picked a rose for his Zelinda.

Mercy! Scarcely had he pulled the flower from the stalk when there arose a great noise, and flames darted from the earth, and all at once there appeared a terrible monster with the figure of a dragon, and hissed with all his might, and cried out, enraged at that poor Christian, "Rash man! what have you done? Now you must die at once, for you have had the audacity to touch and destroy my rosebush."

The poor man, more than half dead with terror, began to weep and beg for mercy on his knees, asking pardon for the fault he had committed, and told why he had picked the rose; and then he added, "Let me depart; I have a family, and if I am killed they will go to destruction."

Beauty in the enchanted palace.
Beauty and the Beast, 1811.
Illustrator Unknown

La Belle et la Bête
Contes De Fees, 1908.
Illustrated by Beauge Bertall

But the monster, more wicked than ever, responded, "Listen; one must die. Either bring me the girl that asked for the rose or I will kill you this very moment." It was impossible to move him by prayers or lamentations; the monster persisted in his decision, and did not let the poor man go until he had sworn to bring him there in the garden his daughter Zelinda.

Imagine how downhearted that poor man returned home! He gave his oldest daughters their presents and Zelinda her rose; but his face was distorted and as white as though he had arisen from the dead; so that the girls, in terror, asked him what had happened and whether he had met with any misfortune. They were urgent, and at last the poor man, weeping bitterly, related the misfortunes of that unhappy journey and on what condition he had been able finally to return home. "In short," he exclaimed, "either Zelinda or I must be eaten alive by the monster."

Then the two sisters emptied the vials of their wrath on Zelinda. "Just see," they said, "that affected, capricious girl! She shall go to the monster! She who wanted roses at this season. No, indeed! Papa must stay with us. The stupid creature!"

At all these taunts Zelinda, without growing angry, simply said, "It is right that the one who has caused the misfortune should pay for it. I will go to the monster's. Yes, Papa, take me to the garden, and the Lord's will be done."

The next day Zelinda and her sorrowful father began their journey and at nightfall arrived at the garden gate. When they entered they saw as usual no one, but they beheld a lordly palace all lighted and the doors wide open. When the two travelers entered the vestibule, suddenly four marble statues, with lighted torches in their hands, descended from their pedestals, and accompanied them up the stairs to a large hall where a table was lavishly spread. The travellers, who were very hungry, sat down and began to eat without ceremony; and when they

In the morning Beauty said goodbye to her weeping father.
Beauty and the Beast, 1875.
Illustrated by Eleanor Vere Boyle

had finished, the same statues conducted them to two handsome chambers for the night. Zelinda and her father were so weary that they slept like dormice all night.

At daybreak Zelinda and her father arose, and were served with everything for breakfast by invisible hands. Then they descended to the garden, and began to seek the monster. When they came to the rosebush he appeared in all his frightful ugliness. Zelinda, on seeing him, became pale with fear, and her limbs trembled, but the monster regarded her attentively with his great fiery eyes, and afterward said to the poor man, "Very well; you have kept your word, and I am satisfied. Now depart and leave me alone here with the young girl."

At this command the old man thought he should die; and Zelinda, too, stood there half stupefied and her eyes full of tears; but entreaties were of no avail; the monster remained as obdurate as a stone, and the poor man was obliged to depart, leaving his dear Zelinda in the monster's power.

When the monster was alone with Zelinda he began to caress her, and make loving speeches to her, and managed to appear quite civil. There was no danger of his forgetting her, and he saw that she wanted nothing, and every day, talking with her in the garden, he asked her, "Do you love me, Zelinda? Will you be my wife?"

The young girl always answered him in the same way, "I like you, sir, but I will never be your wife."

Then the monster appeared very sorrowful, and redoubled his caresses and attentions, and, sighing deeply, said, "But you see, Zelinda, if you should marry me wonderful things would happen. What they are I cannot tell you until you will be my wife."

The Beast appeared suddenly from behind a curtain.
My Book of Favourite Fairy Tales, 1921.
Illustrated by Jennie Harbour

Zelinda, although in her heart not dissatisfied with that beautiful place and with being treated like a queen, still did not feel at all like marrying the monster, because he was too ugly and looked like a beast, and always answered his requests in the same manner.

One day, however, the monster called Zelinda in haste, and said, "Listen, Zelinda; if you do not consent to marry me it is fated that your father must die. He is ill and near the end of his life, and you will not be able even to see him again. See whether I am telling you the truth." And, drawing out an enchanted mirror, the monster showed Zelinda her father on his deathbed.

At that spectacle Zelinda, in despair and half mad with grief, cried, "Oh, save my father, for mercy's sake! Let me be able to embrace him once more before he dies. Yes, yes, I promise you I will be your faithful and constant wife, and that without delay. But save my father from death."

Scarcely had Zelinda uttered these words when suddenly the monster was transformed into a very handsome youth. Zelinda was astounded by this unexpected change, and the young man took her by the hand, and said, "Know, dear Zelinda, that I am the son of the King of the Oranges. An old witch, touching me, changed me into the terrible monster I was, and condemned me to be hidden in this rosebush until a beautiful girl consented to become my wife."

Beauty's Room.

Beauty and the Beast, 1873.

Illustrated by Walter Crane

THE MAIDEN AND THE BEAST

(A Portuguese Tale)

This tale comes from an anthology of *Portuguese Folk Tales*, compiled by Zófimo Consiglieri Pedroso (1851 – 1910), a Portuguese historian, writer, ethnographer and folklorist. He was devoted to the study of ethnography (the systematic study of people and cultures) and introduced anthropology as an academic pursuit to Portugal, studying the country's myths, popular traditions and superstitions. Ironically, for a book dedicated to Portuguese culture and story-telling, the book was actually issued in England (in 1878) *before* its native publication.

'The Maiden and the Beast' differs from most other 'beauty and the beast' tales in that the youngest daughter does not ask for a rose, but merely wishes for her 'dear father's health.' Pressured, she then asks for 'a slice of roach from a green meadow' – a request which spells disastrous consequences. In this version, the protagonist does not meet the beast until the end of the tale – and there is no 'happy ending' to speak of. The white horse and the sisters' forgetfulness (instead of spite or jealousy) are also new additions, making this narrative rather unique in the *Beauty and the Beast* tradition.

There was once a man who had three daughters; he loved them all, but there was one he loved more than the others. As he was going to the fair one day he inquired what they would like him to bring them. One said she would like to have a hat and some boots, the other one asked for a dress and a shawl, but the one he loved most did not ask for anything. The man, in surprise, said, "Oh! my child, do you not want anything?"

"No, I want nothing; I only wish that my dear father may enjoy health."

"You must ask for something, it matters not what it is, I shall bring it to you," replied the father. But, in order that the father should not continue to importune her, she said, "I wish my father to bring me a slice of roach off a green meadow."

The good man set off to the fair, bought all the things that his daughters had asked him, and searched every where for the "slice of roach off a green meadow," but could not find it, for it was something that was not to be had. He there fore came home in great distress of mind, because she was the daughter he loved most and wished most to please. As he was walking along he happened to see a light shining on the road, and, as it was already night, he walked on and on until he reached the light.

The light came from a hut in which lived a shepherd; the man went in and inquired of him, "Can you tell me what palace is that yonder, and do you think they would give me shelter there?" The shepherd replied, in great astonishment, "Oh! sir, but in that palace no one resides, some thing is seen there which terrifies people from living in it." "What does it matter, it will not eat me up; and, as there is no one living in it, I shall go and sleep there to-night." He went up to the building, found it all lit up very splendidly, and, on entering into the palace, he found a table ready laid.

As he approached the table, he heard a voice which said, "Eat and lie down on the bed which you see there, and in the morning rise and take with you what you will find on that table, which is what your daughter asked you for; but at the end of three days you must bring her here." The man was very pleased to be able to take home what his daughter had asked him for, but at the same time was

Beauty visits her library.

Beauty and the Beast, 1811.

Illustrator Unknown

Beauty was much pleased with them, and asked them to show her bout the palace.
Beauty and the Beast, 1885.
Published by Peter G. Thomson

distressed at what the voice had said it required him to do. He threw himself on the bed, and on the following morning he arose, went straight to the table, and found upon it the slice of roach off a green meadow.

He took it up and went home; the moment he arrived his daughters surrounded him: "Father, what have you brought us? let us see what it is;" the father gave them what he had brought them. The third daughter, the one he loved most, did not ask him for anything, but simply if he was well. The father answered her, "My daughter, I come back both happy and sad! Here you have what you asked me for." "Oh! father, I asked you for this because it was a thing which did not exist; but why do you come back sad?" "Because I must take you at the end of three days to the place where this was given to me." He recounted all that had occurred to him in the place, and what the voice had told him to do. When the daughter heard all she replied, "Do not distress yourself, father, for I shall go, and whatever God wills, will happen."

And so it happened that at the end of three days the father took her to the enchanted palace. It was all illuminated and in a blaze of light; the table was laid, and two beds had been prepared. As they entered they heard a voice saying, "Eat and remain with your daughter three days that she may not feel frightened." The man remained the three days in the palace, and at the end went away leaving the daughter alone! The voice spoke to her every day but no form was seen. At the end of a few days the girl heard a bird singing in the garden. The voice said to her, "Do you hear that bird sing?" "Yes, I hear him," replied the girl, "Does it bring any news?" "It is your eldest sister who is going to be married, would you like to be present?" asked the voice.

The girl in great delight said, "Yes, I should like to go very much,-will you let me go?" "I will allow you," rejoined the voice, "but you will not re turn!" "Yes, I shall come back," said the girl. The voice gave her then a ring so that she should not forget her promise, saying, "Now mind that at the end of three days a white horse will go for you; it will give three knocks,-the first is for you to dress, and get ready, -the second for you to take leave of your family,-and the third for you to mount it. If at the third knock you are not on the horse, it will go away and leave you there." The girl went home. A great feast had been prepared and the sister was married. At the end of three days the white horse came to give the three knocks.

At the first the girl commenced to get ready, at the second knock she took leave of her family, and at the third she mounted on the horse. The voice had given the girl a box with money to take to her father and her sisters; on that account they did not wish her to return to the enchanted palace, because she was now very rich. But the girl remembered what she had promised, and the moment she found herself on the horse she darted off. After a certain time the bird returned and began to sing very contentedly in the garden. The voice said to her, "Do you hear the bird sing?" "Yes I hear it," replied the girl, "Does it bring any news?" "It is that another of your sisters is about to marry; and do you wish to go?" "Yes, I wish to go; and would you allow me to go?" "I will let you go," replied the voice; "but you will not return!" "Yes, I shall return," said the girl.

The voice then said, "Remember that if at the end of three days you do not come back you shall remain there, and you will he the most hapless girl there is in the world!" The girl started off. A great feast was given and the sister was married. At the end of three days the white horse came-it gave the first knock, and the girl dressed herself to go; it gave the second knock, and the girl took leave of her friends; it gave the third knock, and the girl mounted the horse and returned to the palace. After some time the bird again sang in the garden, but in melancholy tones,--very dull tones indeed.

The voice said to her, "Do you hear the bird sing?" "Yes, I hear it," replied the girl: "is there any news?" "Yes, there are; it is that your father is dying, and does not wish to die without taking leave of you." "And will you allow me to go

From this time the monkeys always waited upon her.

Beauty and the Beast, 1873.

Illustrated by Walter Crane

and see him?" asked the girl, indeed much distressed. "Yes, I will let you go; but I know you will not return this time." "Oh yes, I shall come back," replied the girl. The voice then said to her, "No, you will not return--you will not! for your sisters will not let you come; you and they will be the most unhappy girls in this world if' you do not come back at the end of three days."

The girl went home, the father was very ill, yet he could not die until he saw her, and he had hardly taken leave of his daughter when he died. The sisters gave the girl a sleeping draught as she had requested them, and left her to sleep. The girl had begged them most particularly to awaken her before the white horse should come. What did the sisters do? They did not awaken her, and they took off the ring she wore. At the end of three days the horse came--it gave the first knock; it knocked the second time; it knocked the third time, and went away and the girl remained at home.

As the sisters had taken away the ring, she forgot everything of the past and lived very happily with her sisters. A few days after this fortune began to leave her and her sisters, until one day the two said to her, "Sister, do you remember the white horse?" The girl then recollected everything and began to cry, saying, "Oh I what misfortune is mine, oh! you have made me very wretched what has become of my ring?" The sisters gave her the ring, and the girl took her departure in great affliction. She reached the enchanted palace and found everything about it looking very dull, very dark, and the palace shut up. She went straight into the garden and she there found a huge beast lying on the ground.

The beast had barely seen her when he cried out, "Go away, you tyrant, for you have broken my spell! Now you will be the most wretched girl in the world, you and your sisters." As the beast finished saying this it died. The girl returned to her sisters in great distress, weeping very bitterly, and she remained in the house without eating or drinking, and after a few days died also. The sisters became poorer by degrees for having been the cause of all this trouble.

So tame that they flew to Beauty as soon as they saw her.
The Blue Fairy Book, 1922.
Illustrated by H. J. Ford

May I walk with you, Beauty?
Beauty and the Beast and Other Stories, *c.*1920.
Illustrated by John Hassall

Beauty and the Beast

(An English Tale)

'Beauty and the Beast' was written down by the Scottish folklorist Andrew Lang (1844 - 1912), in *The Blue Fairy Book* (1889). Lang produced twelve collections of fairy tales in total, each volume distinguished by its own colour. Although he did not collect the stories himself from oral primary sources, Lang is only rivalled by Madame d'Aulnoy (1650 - 1705) for the sheer variety of sources and cultural diversity included in his anthologies. Lang's 'Beauty and the Beast' was not the first version to appear in English; that was published by J. R. Planché in 1757.

Lang's tale is a complex mixture of Beaumont and Villeneuve's stories, but encompasses more of the fine details, and character development of Villeneuve. Lang was determined to collate as much original (or as close to original) folkloric storytelling as possible. When he began his efforts, he said that he 'was fighting against the critics and educationalists of the day', who judged the traditional tales' 'unreality, brutality and escapism to be harmful for young readers... [and] beneath the serious consideration of those of mature age.' Over a generation, Lang's books worked a revelation in this public perception, 'Beauty and the Beast' being no exception.

>———→

Once upon a time, in a very far-off country, there lived a merchant who had been so fortunate in all his undertakings that he was enormously rich. As he had, however, six sons and six daughters, he found that his money was not too much to let them all have everything they fancied, as they were accustomed to do.

Every evening the beast paid her a visit
Old Time Stories, 1921.

Illustrated by W. Heath Robinson

But one day a most unexpected misfortune befell them. Their house caught fire and was speedily burnt to the ground, with all the splendid furniture, the books, pictures, gold, silver, and precious goods it contained; and this was only the beginning of their troubles. Their father, who had until this moment prospered in all ways, suddenly lost every ship he had upon the sea, either by dint of pirates, shipwreck, or fire. Then he heard that his clerks in distant countries, whom he trusted entirely, had proved unfaithful; and at last from great wealth he fell into the direst poverty.

All that he had left was a little house in a desolate place at least a hundred leagues from the town in which he had lived, and to this he was forced to retreat with his children, who were in despair at the idea of leading such a different life. Indeed, the daughters at first hoped that their friends, who had been so numerous while they were rich, would insist on their staying in their houses now they no longer possessed one. But they soon found that they were left alone, and that their former friends even attributed their misfortunes to their own extravagance, and showed no intention of offering them any help. So nothing was left for them but to take their departure to the cottage, which stood in the midst of a dark forest, and seemed to be the most dismal place upon the face of the earth. As they were too poor to have any servants, the girls had to work hard, like peasants, and the sons, for their part, cultivated the fields to earn their living. Roughly clothed, and living in the simplest way, the girls regretted unceasingly the luxuries and amusements of their former life; only the youngest tried to be brave and cheerful. She had been as sad as anyone when misfortune overtook her father, but, soon recovering her natural gaiety, she set to work to make the best of things, to amuse her father and brothers as well as she could, and to try to persuade her sisters to join her in dancing and singing. But they would do nothing of the sort, and, because she was not as doleful as themselves, they declared that this miserable life was all she was fit for. But she was really far prettier and cleverer than they were; indeed, she was so lovely that she was always called Beauty. After two years, when they were all beginning to get used to their new life, something happened to disturb their tranquillity. Their father received the news that one of his ships, which he had believed to be lost, had come safely into port with a rich cargo. All the sons and daughters at once thought that their poverty was at an end, and wanted to set out directly for the town; but their father, who was more prudent, begged them to wait a little, and, though it was harvest time, and he could ill be spared, determined to go himself first, to make inquiries. Only the youngest daughter had any doubt but that they would soon again be as rich as they were before, or at least rich enough to live comfortably in some town where they would find amusement and gay companions once more. So they all loaded their father with commissions for jewels and dresses which it would have taken a fortune to buy; only Beauty, feeling sure that it was of no use, did not ask for anything. Her father, noticing her silence, said: "And what shall I bring for you, Beauty?"

"The only thing I wish for is to see you come home safely," she answered.

But this only vexed her sisters, who fancied she was blaming them for having asked for such costly things. Her father, however, was pleased, but as he thought that at her age she certainly ought to like pretty presents, he told her to choose something.

"Well, dear father," she said, "as you insist upon it, I beg that you will bring me a rose. I have not seen one since we came here, and I love them so much."

So the merchant set out and reached the town as quickly as possible, but only to find that his former companions, believing him to be dead, had divided between them the goods which the ship had brought; and after six months of trouble and expense he found himself as poor as when he started, having been able to recover only just enough to pay the cost of his journey. To make matters worse, he was obliged to leave the town in the most terrible weather, so that by the time he was within a few leagues of his home he was almost exhausted with

La Belle et la Bête

Contes De Fees, 1908.

Illustrated by Beauge Bertall

La Belle et la Bête
Contes de Perrault, 1910.
Illustrated by Margaret Tarrant

cold and fatigue. Though he knew it would take some hours to get through the forest, he was so anxious to be at his journey's end that he resolved to go on; but night overtook him, and the deep snow and bitter frost made it impossible for his horse to carry him any further. Not a house was to be seen; the only shelter he could get was the hollow trunk of a great tree, and there he crouched all the night which seemed to him the longest he had ever known. In spite of his weariness the howling of the wolves kept him awake, and even when at last the day broke he was not much better off, for the falling snow had covered up every path, and he did not know which way to turn.

At length he made out some sort of track, and though at the beginning it was so rough and slippery that he fell down more than once, it presently became easier, and led him into an avenue of trees which ended in a splendid castle. It seemed to the merchant very strange that no snow had fallen in the avenue, which was entirely composed of orange trees, covered with flowers and fruit. When he reached the first court of the castle he saw before him a flight of agate steps, and went up them, and passed through several splendidly furnished rooms. The pleasant warmth of the air revived him, and he felt very hungry; but there seemed to be nobody in all this vast and splendid palace whom he could ask to give him something to eat. Deep silence reigned everywhere, and at last, tired of roaming through empty rooms and galleries, he stopped in a room smaller than the rest, where a clear fire was burning and a couch was drawn up closely to it. Thinking that this must be prepared for someone who was expected, he sat down to wait till he should come, and very soon fell into a sweet sleep.

When his extreme hunger wakened him after several hours, he was still alone; but a little table, upon which was a good dinner, had been drawn up close to him, and, as he had eaten nothing for twenty-four hours, he lost no time in beginning his meal, hoping that he might soon have an opportunity of thanking his considerate entertainer, whoever it might be. But no one appeared, and even after another long sleep, from which he awoke completely refreshed, there was no sign of anybody, though a fresh meal of dainty cakes and fruit was prepared upon the little table at his elbow. Being naturally timid, the silence began to terrify him, and he resolved to search once more through all the rooms; but it was of no use. Not even a servant was to be seen; there was no sign of life in the palace! He began to wonder what he should do, and to amuse himself by pretending that all the treasures he saw were his own, and considering how he would divide them among his children. Then he went down into the garden, and though it was winter everywhere else, here the sun shone, and the birds sang, and the flowers bloomed, and the air was soft and sweet. The merchant, in ecstasies with all he saw and heard, said to himself:

"All this must be meant for me. I will go this minute and bring my children to share all these delights."

In spite of being so cold and weary when he reached the castle, he had taken his horse to the stable and fed it. Now he thought he would saddle it for his homeward journey, and he turned down the path which led to the stable. This path had a hedge of roses on each side of it, and the merchant thought he had never seen or smelt such exquisite flowers. They reminded him of his promise to Beauty, and he stopped and had just gathered one to take to her when he was startled by a strange noise behind him. Turning round, he saw a frightful Beast, which seemed to be very angry and said, in a terrible voice:

"Who told you that you might gather my roses? Was it not enough that I allowed you to be in my palace and was kind to you? This is the way you show your gratitude, by stealing my flowers! But your insolence shall not go unpunished." The merchant, terrified by these furious words, dropped the fatal rose, and, throwing himself on his knees, cried: "Pardon me, noble sir. I am truly grateful to you for your hospitality, which was so magnificent that I could not imagine that you would be offended by my taking such a little thing as a rose." But the Beast's anger was not lessened by this speech.

92

Beauty and the Beast
Old, Old Fairy Tales, 1935.
Illustrated by Anne Anderson

Beauty and the Beast
The Now-A-Days Fairy Book, 1922.
Illustrated by Jessie Willcox Smith

"You are very ready with excuses and flattery," he cried; "but that will not save you from the death you deserve."

"Alas!" thought the merchant, "if my daughter could only know what danger her rose has brought me into!"

And in despair he began to tell the Beast all his misfortunes, and the reason of his journey, not forgetting to mention Beauty's request.

"A king's ransom would hardly have procured all that my other daughters asked." he said: "but I thought that I might at least take Beauty her rose. I beg you to forgive me, for you see I meant no harm."

The Beast considered for a moment, and then he said, in a less furious tone:

"I will forgive you on one condition—that is, that you will give me one of your daughters."

"Ah!" cried the merchant, "if I were cruel enough to buy my own life at the expense of one of my children's, what excuse could I invent to bring her here?"

"No excuse would be necessary," answered the Beast. "If she comes at all she must come willingly. On no other condition will I have her. See if any one of them is courageous enough, and loves you well enough to come and save your life. You seem to be an honest man, so I will trust you to go home. I give you a month to see if either of your daughters will come back with you and stay here, to let you go free. If neither of them is willing, you must come alone, after bidding them good-by for ever, for then you will belong to me. And do not imagine that you can hide from me, for if you fail to keep your word I will come and fetch you!" added the Beast grimly.

They talked for a while about things of no great importance.
Beauty and the Beast, 1875.
Illustrated by Eleanor Vere Boyle

The merchant accepted this proposal, though he did not really think any of his daughters could be persuaded to come. He promised to return at the time appointed, and then, anxious to escape from the presence of the Beast, he asked permission to set off at once. But the Beast answered that he could not go until next day.

"Then you will find a horse ready for you," he said. "Now go and eat your supper, and await my orders."

The poor merchant, more dead than alive, went back to his room, where the most delicious supper was already served on the little table which was drawn up before a blazing fire. But he was too terrified to eat, and only tasted a few of the dishes, for fear the Beast should be angry if he did not obey his orders. When he had finished he heard a great noise in the next room, which he knew meant that the Beast was coming. As he could do nothing to escape his visit, the only thing that remained was to seem as little afraid as possible; so when the Beast appeared and asked roughly if he had supped well, the merchant answered humbly that he had, thanks to his host's kindness. Then the Beast warned him to remember their agreement, and to prepare his daughter exactly for what she had to expect.

"Do not get up to-morrow," he added, "until you see the sun and hear a golden bell ring. Then you will find your breakfast waiting for you here, and the horse you are to ride will be ready in the courtyard. He will also bring you back again when you come with your daughter a month hence. Farewell. Take a rose to Beauty, and remember your promise!"

The merchant was only too glad when the Beast went away, and though he could not sleep for sadness, he lay down until the sun rose. Then, after a hasty breakfast, he went to gather Beauty's rose, and mounted his horse, which carried him off so swiftly that in an instant he had lost sight of the palace, and he was still wrapped in gloomy thoughts when it stopped before the door of the cottage.

His sons and daughters, who had been very uneasy at his long absence, rushed to meet him, eager to know the result of his journey, which, seeing him mounted upon a splendid horse and wrapped in a rich mantle, they supposed to be favourable. He hid the truth from them at first, only saying sadly to Beauty as he gave her the rose:

"Here is what you asked me to bring you; you little know what it has cost."

But this excited their curiosity so greatly that presently he told them his adventures from beginning to end, and then they were all very unhappy. The girls lamented loudly over their lost hopes, and the sons declared that their father should not return to this terrible castle, and began to make plans for killing the Beast if it should come to fetch him. But he reminded them that he had promised to go back. Then the girls were very angry with Beauty, and said it was all her fault, and that if she had asked for something sensible this would never have happened, and complained bitterly that they should have to suffer for her folly.

Poor Beauty, much distressed, said to them:

"I have, indeed, caused this misfortune, but I assure you I did it innocently. Who could have guessed that to ask for a rose in the middle of summer would cause so much misery? But as I did the mischief it is only just that I should suffer for it. I will therefore go back with my father to keep his promise."

At first nobody would hear of this arrangement, and her father and brothers, who loved her dearly, declared that nothing should make them let her go; but Beauty was firm. As the time drew near she divided all her little possessions

The poor Beast sat spellbound listening to Beauty's music.
Nursery Tales, 1923.
Illustrated by Paul Woodroffe

between her sisters, and said good-by to everything she loved, and when the fatal day came she encouraged and cheered her father as they mounted together the horse which had brought him back. It seemed to fly rather than gallop, but so smoothly that Beauty was not frightened; indeed, she would have enjoyed the journey if she had not feared what might happen to her at the end of it. Her father still tried to persuade her to go back, but in vain. While they were talking the night fell, and then, to their great surprise, wonderful coloured lights began to shine in all directions, and splendid fireworks blazed out before them; all the forest was illuminated by them, and even felt pleasantly warm, though it had been bitterly cold before. This lasted until they reached the avenue of orange trees, where were statues holding flaming torches, and when they got nearer to the palace they saw that it was illuminated from the roof to the ground, and music sounded softly from the courtyard. "The Beast must be very hungry," said Beauty, trying to laugh, "if he makes all this rejoicing over the arrival of his prey."

But, in spite of her anxiety, she could not help admiring all the wonderful things she saw.

The horse stopped at the foot of the flight of steps leading to the terrace, and when they had dismounted her father led her to the little room he had been in before, where they found a splendid fire burning, and the table daintily spread with a delicious supper.

The merchant knew that this was meant for them, and Beauty, who was rather less frightened now that she had passed through so many rooms and seen nothing of the Beast, was quite willing to begin, for her long ride had made her very hungry. But they had hardly finished their meal when the noise of the Beast's footsteps was heard approaching, and Beauty clung to her father in terror, which became all the greater when she saw how frightened he was. But when the Beast really appeared, though she trembled at the sight of him,

In her dreams a kindly lady appeared and told her to have no fears.

Beauty and the Beast, 1875.

Illustrated by Eleanor Vere Boyle

she made a great effort to hide her terror, and saluted him respectfully.

This evidently pleased the Beast. After looking at her he said, in a tone that might have struck terror into the boldest heart, though he did not seem to be angry:

"Good-evening, old man. Good-evening, Beauty."

The merchant was too terrified to reply, but Beauty answered sweetly: "Good-evening, Beast."

"Have you come willingly?" asked the Beast. "Will you be content to stay here when your father goes away?"

Beauty answered bravely that she was quite prepared to stay.

"I am pleased with you," said the Beast. "As you have come of your own accord, you may stay. As for you, old man," he added, turning to the merchant, "at sunrise to-morrow you will take your departure. When the bell rings get up quickly and eat your breakfast, and you will find the same horse waiting to take you home; but remember that you must never expect to see my palace again."

Then turning to Beauty, he said:

"Take your father into the next room, and help him to choose everything you think your brothers and sisters would like to have. You will find two travelling-trunks there; fill them as full as you can. It is only just that you should send them something very precious as a remembrance of yourself."

Then he went away, after saying, "Good-by, Beauty; good-by, old man"; and though Beauty was beginning to think with great dismay of her father's

Beauty found her dreams so interesting that she was in no hurry to awake.
The Blue Fairy Book, 1922.
Illustrated by H. J. Ford

Every evening at supper he would ask the old question, "Beauty, will you marry me?"
And always she replied, in a very decided way, "No, Beast"

Fairy Tales, 1915.

Illustrated by Margaret Tarrant

departure, she was afraid to disobey the Beast's orders; and they went into the next room, which had shelves and cupboards all round it. They were greatly surprised at the riches it contained. There were splendid dresses fit for a queen, with all the ornaments that were to be worn with them; and when Beauty opened the cupboards she was quite dazzled by the gorgeous jewels that lay in heaps upon every shelf. After choosing a vast quantity, which she divided between her sisters—for she had made a heap of the wonderful dresses for each of them—she opened the last chest, which was full of gold.

"I think, father," she said, "that, as the gold will be more useful to you, we had better take out the other things again, and fill the trunks with it." So they did this; but the more they put in the more room there seemed to be, and at last they put back all the jewels and dresses they had taken out, and Beauty even added as many more of the jewels as she could carry at once; and then the trunks were not too full, but they were so heavy that an elephant could not have carried them!

"The Beast was mocking us," cried the merchant; "he must have pretended to give us all these things, knowing that I could not carry them away."

"Let us wait and see," answered Beauty. "I cannot believe that he meant to deceive us. All we can do is to fasten them up and leave them ready."

So they did this and returned to the little room, where, to their astonishment, they found breakfast ready. The merchant ate his with a good appetite, as the Beast's generosity made him believe that he might perhaps venture to come back soon and see Beauty. But she felt sure that her father was leaving her for ever, so she was very sad when the bell rang sharply for the second time, and warned them that the time had come for them to part. They went down into the courtyard, where two horses were waiting, one loaded with the two trunks, the other for him to ride. They were pawing the ground in their impatience

Am I so very ugly?
Beauty and the Beast, 1885.
Published by Peter G. Thomson

to start, and the merchant was forced to bid Beauty a hasty farewell; and as soon as he was mounted he went off at such a pace that she lost sight of him in an instant. Then Beauty began to cry, and wandered sadly back to her own room. But she soon found that she was very sleepy, and as she had nothing better to do she lay down and instantly fell asleep. And then she dreamed that she was walking by a brook bordered with trees, and lamenting her sad fate, when a young prince, handsomer than anyone she had ever seen, and with a voice that went straight to her heart, came and said to her, "Ah, Beauty! you are not so unfortunate as you suppose. Here you will be rewarded for all you have suffered elsewhere. Your every wish shall be gratified. Only try to find me out, no matter how I may be disguised, as I love you dearly, and in making me happy you will find your own happiness. Be as true-hearted as you are beautiful, and we shall have nothing left to wish for."

"What can I do, Prince, to make you happy?" said Beauty.

"Only be grateful," he answered, "and do not trust too much to your eyes. And, above all, do not desert me until you have saved me from my cruel misery."

After this she thought she found herself in a room with a stately and beautiful lady, who said to her:

"Dear Beauty, try not to regret all you have left behind you, for you are destined to a better fate. Only do not let yourself be deceived by appearances."

Beauty found her dreams so interesting that she was in no hurry to awake, but presently the clock roused her by calling her name softly twelve times, and then she got up and found her dressing-table set out with everything she could possibly want; and when her toilet was finished she found dinner was waiting in the room next to hers. But dinner does not take very long when you are all by yourself, and very soon she sat down cosily in the corner of a sofa, and began to think about the charming Prince she had seen in her dream.

"He said I could make him happy," said Beauty to herself.

"It seems, then, that this horrible Beast keeps him a prisoner. How can I set him free? I wonder why they both told me not to trust to appearances? I don't understand it. But, after all, it was only a dream, so why should I trouble myself about it? I had better go and find something to do to amuse myself."

So she got up and began to explore some of the many rooms of the palace.

The first she entered was lined with mirrors, and Beauty saw herself reflected on every side, and thought she had never seen such a charming room. Then a bracelet which was hanging from a chandelier caught her eye, and on taking it down she was greatly surprised to find that it held a portrait of her unknown admirer, just as she had seen him in her dream. With great delight she slipped the bracelet on her arm, and went on into a gallery of pictures, where she soon found a portrait of the same handsome Prince, as large as life, and so well painted that as she studied it he seemed to smile kindly at her. Tearing herself away from the portrait at last, she passed through into a room which contained every musical instrument under the sun, and here she amused herself for a long while in trying some of them, and singing until she was tired. The next room was a library, and she saw everything she had ever wanted to read, as well as everything she had read, and it seemed to her that a whole lifetime would not be enough to even read the names of the books, there were so many. By this time it was growing dusk, and wax candles in diamond and ruby candlesticks were beginning to light themselves in every room.

Beauty found her supper served just at the time she preferred to have it, but she did not see anyone or hear a sound, and, though her father had warned her that she would be alone, she began to find it rather dull.

Am I so very ugly?

Beauty and the Beast, 1873.

Illustrated by Walter Crane

But presently she heard the Beast coming, and wondered tremblingly if he meant to eat her up now.

However, as he did not seem at all ferocious, and only said gruffly:

"Good-evening, Beauty," she answered cheerfully and managed to conceal her terror. Then the Beast asked her how she had been amusing herself, and she told him all the rooms she had seen.

Then he asked if she thought she could be happy in his palace; and Beauty answered that everything was so beautiful that she would be very hard to please if she could not be happy. And after about an hour's talk Beauty began to think that the Beast was not nearly so terrible as she had supposed at first. Then he got up to leave her, and said in his gruff voice:

"Do you love me, Beauty? Will you marry me?"

"Oh! what shall I say?" cried Beauty, for she was afraid to make the Beast angry by refusing.

"Say 'yes' or 'no' without fear," he replied.

"Oh! no, Beast," said Beauty hastily.

"Since you will not, good-night, Beauty," he said.

And she answered, "Good-night, Beast," very glad to find that her refusal had not provoked him. And after he was gone she was very soon in bed and asleep, and dreaming of her unknown Prince. She thought he came and said to her:

Beauty sees her father in the looking-glass.
The Big Book of Fairy Tales, 1911.
Illustrated by Charles Robinson

She woke the following morning in her father's cottage.
Beauty and the Beast, 1875.
Illustrated by Eleanor Vere Boyle

"Ah, Beauty! why are you so unkind to me? I fear I am fated to be unhappy for many a long day still."

And then her dreams changed, but the charming Prince figured in them all; and when morning came her first thought was to look at the portrait, and see if it was really like him, and she found that it certainly was.

This morning she decided to amuse herself in the garden, for the sun shone, and all the fountains were playing; but she was astonished to find that every place was familiar to her, and presently she came to the brook where the myrtle trees were growing where she had first met the Prince in her dream, and that made her think more than ever that he must be kept a prisoner by the Beast. When she was tired she went back to the palace, and found a new room full of materials for every kind of work—ribbons to make into bows, and silks to work into flowers. Then there was an aviary full of rare birds, which were so tame that they flew to Beauty as soon as they saw her, and perched upon her shoulders and her head.

"Pretty little creatures," she said, "how I wish that your cage was nearer to my room, that I might often hear you sing!"

So saying she opened a door, and found, to her delight, that it led into her own room, though she had thought it was quite the other side of the palace.

There were more birds in a room farther on, parrots and cockatoos that could talk, and they greeted Beauty by name; indeed, she found them so entertaining that she took one or two back to her room, and they talked to her while she was at supper; after which the Beast paid her his usual visit, and asked her the same questions as before, and then with a gruff "good-night" he took his departure, and Beauty went to bed to dream of her mysterious Prince. The days passed swiftly in different amusements, and after a while Beauty found out another strange thing in the palace, which often pleased her when she was tired of being alone. There was one room which she had not noticed particularly; it was empty, except that under each of the windows stood a very comfortable chair; and the first time she had looked out of the window it had seemed to her that a black curtain prevented her from seeing anything outside. But the second time she went into the room, happening to be tired, she sat down in one of the chairs, when instantly the curtain was rolled aside, and a most amusing pantomime was acted before her; there were dances, and coloured lights, and music, and pretty dresses, and it was all so gay that Beauty was in ecstasies. After that she tried the other seven windows in turn, and there was some new and surprising entertainment to be seen from each of them, so that Beauty never could feel lonely any more. Every evening after supper the Beast came to see her, and always before saying good-night asked her in his terrible voice:

"Beauty, will you marry me?"

And it seemed to Beauty, now she understood him better, that when she said, "No, Beast," he went away quite sad. But her happy dreams of the handsome young Prince soon made her forget the poor Beast, and the only thing that at all disturbed her was to be constantly told to distrust appearances, to let her heart guide her, and not her eyes, and many other equally perplexing things, which, consider as she would, she could not understand.

So everything went on for a long time, until at last, happy as she was, Beauty began to long for the sight of her father and her brothers and sisters; and one night, seeing her look very sad, the Beast asked her what was the matter. Beauty had quite ceased to be afraid of him. Now she knew that he was really gentle in spite of his ferocious looks and his dreadful voice. So she answered that she was longing to see her home once more. Upon hearing this the Beast seemed sadly distressed, and cried miserably.

At last she remembered her dream, rushed to the grass-plot,
and there saw him lying apparently dead.

The Fairy Book, 1923.

Illustrated by Warwick Goble

"Ah! Beauty, have you the heart to desert an unhappy Beast like this? What more do you want to make you happy? Is it because you hate me that you want to escape?"

"No, dear Beast," answered Beauty softly, "I do not hate you, and I should be very sorry never to see you any more, but I long to see my father again. Only let me go for two months, and I promise to come back to you and stay for the rest of my life."

The Beast, who had been sighing dolefully while she spoke, now replied:

"I cannot refuse you anything you ask, even though it should cost me my life. Take the four boxes you will find in the room next to your own, and fill them with everything you wish to take with you. But remember your promise and come back when the two months are over, or you may have cause to repent it, for if you do not come in good time you will find your faithful Beast dead. You will not need any chariot to bring you back. Only say good-by to all your brothers and sisters the night before you come away, and when you have gone to bed turn this ring round upon your finger and say firmly: 'I wish to go back to my palace and see my Beast again.' Good-night, Beauty. Fear nothing, sleep peacefully, and before long you shall see your father once more."

As soon as Beauty was alone she hastened to fill the boxes with all the rare and precious things she saw about her, and only when she was tired of heaping things into them did they seem to be full.

Then she went to bed, but could hardly sleep for joy. And when at last she did begin to dream of her beloved Prince she was grieved to see him stretched upon a grassy bank, sad and weary, and hardly like himself.

"What is the matter?" she cried.

*At length she found poor Beast stretched out on the grass-plot,
close to the fountain, to all appearance dead.*

Fairy Tales, 1915.

Illustrated by Margaret Tarrant

He looked at her reproachfully, and said:

"How can you ask me, cruel one? Are you not leaving me to my death perhaps?"

"Ah! don't be so sorrowful," cried Beauty; "I am only going to assure my father that I am safe and happy. I have promised the Beast faithfully that I will come back, and he would die of grief if I did not keep my word!"

"What would that matter to you?" said the Prince "Surely you would not care?"

"Indeed, I should be ungrateful if I did not care for such a kind Beast," cried Beauty indignantly. "I would die to save him from pain. I assure you it is not his fault that he is so ugly."

Just then a strange sound woke her—someone was speaking not very far away; and opening her eyes she found herself in a room she had never seen before, which was certainly not nearly so splendid as those she was used to in the Beast's palace. Where could she be? She got up and dressed hastily, and then saw that the boxes she had packed the night before were all in the room. While she was wondering by what magic the Beast had transported them and herself to this strange place she suddenly heard her father's voice, and rushed out and greeted him joyfully. Her brothers and sisters were all astonished at her appearance, as they had never expected to see her again, and there was no end to the questions they asked her. She had also much to hear about what had happened to them while she was away, and of her father's journey home. But when they heard that she had only come to be with them for a short time, and then must go back to the Beast's palace for ever, they lamented loudly. Then Beauty asked her father what he thought could be the meaning of her strange dreams, and why the Prince constantly begged her not to trust to appearances.

The beast dying.
Beauty and the Beast, 1885.
Published by Peter G. Thomson

Beauty and the Beast.
Four and Twenty Fairy Tales, 1858.
Illustrated by Edward Corbould

After much consideration, he answered: "You tell me yourself that the Beast, frightful as he is, loves you dearly, and deserves your love and gratitude for his gentleness and kindness; I think the Prince must mean you to understand that you ought to reward him by doing as he wishes you to, in spite of his ugliness."

Beauty could not help seeing that this seemed very probable; still, when she thought of her dear Prince who was so handsome, she did not feel at all inclined to marry the Beast. At any rate, for two months she need not decide, but could enjoy herself with her sisters. But though they were rich now, and lived in town again, and had plenty of acquaintances, Beauty found that nothing amused her very much; and she often thought of the palace, where she was so happy, especially as at home she never once dreamed of her dear Prince, and she felt quite sad without him.

Then her sisters seemed to have got quite used to being without her, and even found her rather in the way, so she would not have been sorry when the two months were over but for her father and brothers, who begged her to stay, and seemed so grieved at the thought of her departure that she had not the courage to say good-by to them. Every day when she got up she meant to say it at night, and when night came she put it off again, until at last she had a dismal dream which helped her to make up her mind. She thought she was wandering in a lonely path in the palace gardens, when she heard groans which seemed to come from some bushes hiding the entrance of a cave, and running quickly to see what could be the matter, she found the Beast stretched out upon his side, apparently dying. He reproached her faintly with being the cause of his distress, and at the same moment a stately lady appeared, and said very gravely:

"Ah! Beauty, you are only just in time to save his life. See what happens when people do not keep their promises! If you had delayed one day more, you would have found him dead."

Beauty was so terrified by this dream that the next morning she announced her intention of going back at once, and that very night she said good-by to her father and all her brothers and sisters, and as soon as she was in bed she turned her ring round upon her finger, and said firmly, "I wish to go back to my palace and see my Beast again," as she had been told to do.

Then she fell asleep instantly, and only woke up to hear the clock saying "Beauty, Beauty" twelve times in its musical voice, which told her at once that she was really in the palace once more. Everything was just as before, and her birds were so glad to see her! But Beauty thought she had never known such a long day, for she was so anxious to see the Beast again that she felt as if suppertime would never come.

But when it did come and no Beast appeared she was really frightened; so, after listening and waiting for a long time, she ran down into the garden to search for him. Up and down the paths and avenues ran poor Beauty, calling him in vain, for no one answered, and not a trace of him could she find; until at last, quite tired, she stopped for a minute's rest, and saw that she was standing opposite the shady path she had seen in her dream. She rushed down it, and, sure enough, there was the cave, and in it lay the Beast—asleep, as Beauty thought. Quite glad to have found him, she ran up and stroked his head, but, to her horror, he did not move or open his eyes.

"Oh! he is dead; and it is all my fault," said Beauty, crying bitterly.

But then, looking at him again, she fancied he still breathed, and, hastily fetching some water from the nearest fountain, she sprinkled it over his face, and, to her great delight, he began to revive.

"Oh! Beast, how you frightened me!" she cried. "I never knew how much I loved you until just now, when I feared I was too late to save your life."

You broke your promise. I have missed you so badly and now I am close to death.
Beauty and the Beast, 1875.
Illustrated by Eleanor Vere Boyle

The poor Beast was lying senseless on his back.

Beauty and the Beast, 1873.

Illustrated by Walter Crane

"Can you really love such an ugly creature as I am?" said the Beast faintly. "Ah! Beauty, you only came just in time. I was dying because I thought you had forgotten your promise. But go back now and rest, I shall see you again by and by."

Beauty, who had half expected that he would be angry with her, was reassured by his gentle voice, and went back to the palace, where supper was awaiting her; and afterward the Beast came in as usual, and talked about the time she had spent with her father, asking if she had enjoyed herself, and if they had all been very glad to see her.

Beauty answered politely, and quite enjoyed telling him all that had happened to her. And when at last the time came for him to go, and he asked, as he had so often asked before, "Beauty, will you marry me?"

She answered softly, "Yes, dear Beast."

As she spoke a blaze of light sprang up before the windows of the palace; fireworks crackled and guns banged, and across the avenue of orange trees, in letters all made of fire-flies, was written: "Long live the Prince and his Bride."

Turning to ask the Beast what it could all mean, Beauty found that he had disappeared, and in his place stood her long-loved Prince! At the same moment the wheels of a chariot were heard upon the terrace, and two ladies entered the room. One of them Beauty recognized as the stately lady she had seen in her dreams; the other was also so grand and queenly that Beauty hardly knew which to greet first.

But the one she already knew said to her companion:

"Well, Queen, this is Beauty, who has had the courage to rescue your son

125

from the terrible enchantment. They love one another, and only your consent to their marriage is wanting to make them perfectly happy."

"I consent with all my heart," cried the Queen. "How can I ever thank you enough, charming girl, for having restored my dear son to his natural form?"

And then she tenderly embraced Beauty and the Prince, who had meanwhile been greeting the Fairy and receiving her congratulations.

"Now," said the Fairy to Beauty, "I suppose you would like me to send for all your brothers and sisters to dance at your wedding?"

And so she did, and the marriage was celebrated the very next day with the utmost splendour, and Beauty and the Prince lived happily ever after.

The absence of Beauty lamented.
Beauty and the Beast, 1811.
Illustrator Unknown

Ah! What a fright you have given me! She murmured.
The Sleeping Beauty and Other Fairy Tales From the Old French, 1910.
Illustrated by Edmund Dulac

THE FAIRY SERPENT

(A Chinese Tale)

'The Fairy Serpent' was published in Adele M. Fielde's *Chinese Nights Entertainment; Forty Stories told by Almond-Eyed Folk,* a text which appeared in 1893. As Fielde recounted, 'these tales have been heard *or overheard* by the writer, as they were told in the Swatow vernacular, by persons who could not read.' *Swatow,* or 'Shàntóu' is a city on the eastern coast of the Guangdong province of China, particularly significant during the nineteenth century as one of the treaty ports established for Western trade and contact.

Adele M. Fielde (1839 - 1916) was a Baptist missionary to China, whose 'dancing, card-playing and associations with the diplomatic community' resulted in her estrangement from her evangelical peers. Her version of the Chinese tale of 'The Fairy Serpent' most likely derives from the ancient Indian text, the *Panchatantra;* a collection of interrelated animal fables in verse and prose. The original Sanskrit work, which some scholars believe was composed around the 3rd century BCE contained the narrative of 'The Woman Who Married a Snake' – of which obvious parallels are seen in this narrative. In all early societies, young girls were given in marriage by their fathers, and would have very often had to 'learn to love' men who first appeared as 'monsters.'

Oh! He is dead; and it's all my fault.
The Blue Fairy Book, 1922.
Illustrated by H. J. Ford

Once there was a man who had three daughters, of whom he was devotedly fond. They were skilful in embroidery; and he used every day on his way home from work to gather some flowers for them to use as patterns.

One day when he found no flowers along his route homeward he went into the woods to look for wild blossoms, and he unwittingly invaded the domain of a fairy serpent, that coiled around him, held him tightly, and railed at him for having entered his garden. The man excused himself, saying that he came merely to get a few flowers for his daughters, who would be sorely disappointed were he to go home without his usual gift to them.

The snake asked him the number, the names, and the ages of his daughters, and then refused to let him go unless he promised one of them in marriage to him.

The poor man tried every argument he could think of to induce the snake to release him upon easier terms, but the reptile would accept no other ransom. At last the father, dreading greater evil to his daughters should they be deprived of his protection, gave the required promise and went home. He could eat no supper, however, for he knew the power of fairies to afflict those who offend them, and he was full of anxiety concerning the misfortunes that must overwhelm his whole family should the compact be disregarded.

Some days passed; his daughters carefully prepared his meals, and affectionately besought him to eat them, but he would not come to the table. He was always plunged in sorrowful meditation.

They conferred among themselves as to the cause of his uncommon behaviour, and, having decided that one of them must have displeased him, they agreed to try to find out which one it might be, by going separately, each in turn, to urge him to eat.

The eldest went, expressed her distress at his loss of appetite, and urged him to partake of food.

He replied that he would do so if she would for his sake marry the snake to whom he had promised a wife.

She bluntly refused to carry out her father's contract, and left him in deeper trouble than before.

The second daughter then went to beg him to take food, received the same reply, and likewise declined meeting the engagement he had made.

The youngest daughter then went and entreated him to eat, heard his story, and at once declared that, if he would care for his own health properly, she would become the bride of the serpent. The father therefore took his meals again, the days sped without bringing calamity, and the welfare of the family for a time seemed secure.

But one morning, as the girls were sitting at their embroidery, a wasp flew into the room and sang:

> "Buzz! I buzz and come the faster;
> Who will wed the snake, my master?

Whenever the wasp alighted the girls prodded him with their needles, and followed him up so closely that he had to flee for his life. The next morning two wasps came, singing the same refrain; the third morning three wasps came; and the number of wasps increased day by day, until the girls could no longer put them to rout, nor endure their stings.

The Beast split in two and out came the most handsome young prince.
European Folk and Fairy Tales, 1913.
Illustrated by John D. Batten

Then the youngest said that, in order to relieve the family of the buzzing plague, she would go to her uncanny bridegroom. The wasps accompanied her on the road, and guided her into the woods where the fairy serpent awaited her in a palace that he had built for her reception. There were spacious rooms with carved furniture inlaid with precious stones, chests full of silken fabrics, caskets of jade, and jewels of gold.

The snake had beautiful eyes and a musical voice; but his skin was warty, and the girl shuddered at the thought of daily seeing him about. After the wedding supper, at which the two sat alone, the girl told her spouse that she appreciated the excellence of all that he had provided for her, and that she should perform all her domestic duties exactly. For many days she kept the house neat, cooked the food, and made all things pleasant for her repulsive bridegroom. He doted upon her, and pined whenever she was out of his sight. So heedful was he of her wishes and her welfare, that she grew to like his companionship, and to feel a great lonesomeness whenever he was absent.

Having no help in her household work, she was, one day, on finding the well dried up, obliged to go into the forest in search of water, which she finally discovered and toilsomely brought back from a distant spring. On returning she found the snake dying of thirst, and in her eagerness to save his life she grasped and plunged him into the water, from which he rose transformed, a strong and handsome man. He had been the subject of wicked enchantment, from which her dutiful quest and gracious pity set him free. Thereafter she often with her admirable husband visited her old home and carried gifts to those who were less happy than she.

The Beast turns into a prince.
Beauty and the Beast and Other Stories, *c.*1920.
Illustrated by John Hassall

At her feet the handsomest prince that was ever seen.
The Big Book of Fairy Tales, 1911.
Illustrated by Charles Robinson

The Enchanted Tsarévich

(A Russian Tale)

'The Enchanted Tsarévich' was written down by Leonard Arthur Magnus (1879 - 1924) in *Russian Folk Tales,* first published in 1916. Magnus was a linguist, writer and translator who specialised in Russian literature, though he also had a profound interest in Japanese culture. According to his *Times* obituary, Magnus died in Moscow, whilst travelling through Russia in order to collect folktales and folklore for a sequel to his extant edition.

In this version, similarly to the story of 'Zelinda and the Monster', the father is a merchant with three daughters. This time though, the monster is a terrifying winged snake, as usual requesting the father's youngest daughter after catching him picking a beautiful rose. When the young girl is living in the castle, each night the snake asks her to draw his bed a little closer; outside her door, in her room – and finally in her bed. In both *La Belle et La Bête* and *The Enchanted Tsarévich,* the young woman recognises her love for 'the beast' and readily agrees to marriage (unlike Zelinda, the only protagonist to assent only when her father's life is in peril). Of all the tales though, 'The Enchanted Tsarévich' has the most overt sexual content – a young (virginal) girl, given to a phallic creature who forces her to share her bed.

⟶

Once upon a time there was a merchant who had three daughters. It so happened he had one day to go to strange countries to buy wares, and so he asked his daughters, "What shall I bring you from beyond the seas?"

The eldest asked for a new coat, and the next one also asked for a new coat; but the youngest one only took a sheet of paper and sketched a flower on it. "Bring me, *bátyushka* [father], a flower like this!"

So the merchant went and made a long journey to foreign kingdoms, but he could never see such a flower. So he came back home, and he saw on his way a splendid lofty palace with watchtowers, turrets, and a garden. He went a walk in the garden, and you cannot imagine how many trees he saw and flowers, every flower fairer than the other flowers. And then he looked and he saw a single one like the one which his daughter had sketched.

"Oh," he said, "I will tear off and bring this to my beloved daughter; evidently there is nobody here to watch me."

So he ran up and broke it off, and as soon as he had done it, in that very instant a boisterous wind arose and thunder thundered, and a fearful monster stood in front of him, a formless, winged snake with three heads. "How dared you play the master in my garden!" cried the snake to the merchant. "Why have you broken off a blossom?"

The merchant was frightened, fell on his knees and besought pardon.

"Very well," said the snake, "I will forgive you, but on condition that whoever meets you first, when you reach home, you must give me for all eternity; and, if you deceive me, do not forget, nobody can ever hide himself from me. I shall find you wherever you are."

The merchant agreed to the condition and came back home. And the youngest daughter saw him from the window and ran out to meet him. Then

You shall be my bride and later my Queen.

Beauty and the Beast, 1875.

Illustrated by Eleanor Vere Boyle

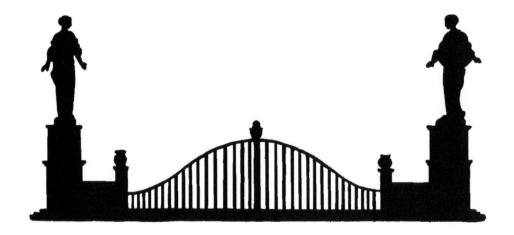

You shall become two statues.

The Big Book of Fairy Tales, 1911.

Illustrated by Charles Robinson

the merchant hung his head, looked at his beloved daughter, and began to shed bitter tears.

"What is the matter with you? Why are you weeping, *bátyushka?*"

He gave her the blossom and told what had befallen him.

"Do not grieve, *bátyushka*," said the youngest daughter. "It is God's gift. Perhaps I shall fare well. Take me to the snake."

So the father took her away, set her in the palace, bade farewell, and set out home. Then the fair maiden, the daughter of the merchant, went in the different rooms, and beheld everywhere gold and velvet; but no one was there to be seen, not a single human soul.

Time went by and went by, and the fair damsel became hungry and thought, "Oh, if I could only have something to eat!" But before ever she had thought, in front of her stood a table, and on the table were dishes and drinks and refreshments. The only thing that was not there was birds' milk. Then she sat down to the table, drank and ate, got up, and it had all vanished.

Darkness now came on, and the merchant's daughter went into the bedroom, wishing to lie down and sleep. Then a boisterous wind rustled round and the three- headed snake appeared in front of her.

"Hail, fair maiden! Put my bed outside this door!"

So the fair maiden put the bed outside the door and herself lay on the bedstead.

She awoke in the morning, and again in the entire house there was not a single soul to be seen. And it all went well with her. Whatever she wished for appeared on the spot.

In the evening the snake flew to her and ordered, "Now, fair maiden, put my bed next to your bedstead."

She then laid it next to her bedstead, and the night went by, and the maiden awoke, and again there was never a soul in the palace.

And for the third time the snake came in the evening and said, "Now, fair maiden, I am going to lie with you in the bedstead."

The merchant's daughter was fearfully afraid of lying on a single bed with such a formless monster. But she could not help herself, so she strengthened her heart and lay down with him.

In the morning the serpent said to her, "If you are now weary, fair maiden, go to your father and your sisters. Spend a day with them, and in the evening come back to me. But see to it that you are not late. If you are one single minute late I shall die of grief."

"No, I shall not be late," said the maiden, the merchant's daughter, and descended the steps; there was a barouche ready for her, and she sat down. That very instant she arrived at her father's courtyard.

Then the father saw, welcomed, kissed her, and asked her, "How has God been dealing with you, my beloved daughter ? Has it been well with you?"

Your doom is to become statues.

Old Time Stories, 1921.

Illustrated by W. Heath Robinson

*Beauty journeyed to the kingdom of the Prince, where they married
and lived ever after in complete happiness.*

Beauty and the Beast, 1875.

Illustrated by Eleanor Vere Boyle

"Very well, father!" And she started telling of all the wealth there was in the palace, how the snake loved her, how whatever she only thought of was in that instant fulfilled.

The sisters heard, and did not know what to do out of sheer envy.

Now the day was ebbing away, and the fair maiden made ready to go back, and was bidding farewell to her father and her sisters, saying, "This is the time I must go back. I was bidden keep to my term."

But the envious sisters rubbed onions on their eyes and made as though they were weeping: "Do not go away, sister; stay until tomorrow."

She was very sorry for her sisters, and stayed one day more.

In the morning she bade farewell to them all and went to the palace. When she arrived it was as empty as before. She went into the garden, and she saw the serpent lying dead in the pond! He had thrown himself for sheer grief into the water.

"Oh, my God, what have I done!" cried out the fair maiden, and she wept bitter tears, ran. up to the pond, hauled the snake out of the water, embraced one head and kissed it with all her might. And the snake trembled, and in a minute turned into a good youth.

"I thank you, fair maiden," he said. "You have saved me from the greatest misfortune. I am no snake, but an enchanted prince."

Then they went back to the merchant's house, were betrothed, lived long, and lived for good and happy things.

THE GOLDEN AGE OF ILLUSTRATION

The 'Golden age of Illustration' refers to a period customarily defined as lasting from the latter quarter of the nineteenth century until just after the First World War. In this period of no more than fifty years the popularity, abundance and most importantly the unprecedented upsurge in quality of illustrated works marked an astounding change in the way that publishers, artists and the general public came to view this hitherto insufficiently esteemed art form.

Until the latter part of the nineteenth century, the work of illustrators was largely proffered anonymously, and in England it was only after Thomas Bewick's pioneering technical advances in wood engraving that it became common to acknowledge the artistic and technical expertise of book and magazine illustrators. Although widely regarded as the patriarch of the *Golden Age*, Walter Crane (1845-1915) started his career as an anonymous illustrator – gradually building his reputation through striking designs, famous for their sharp outlines and flat tints of colour. Like many other great illustrators to follow, Crane operated within many different mediums; a lifelong disciple of William Morris and a member of the Arts and Crafts Movement, he designed all manner of objects including wallpaper, furniture, ceramic ware and even whole interiors. This incredibly important and inclusive phase of British design proved to have a lasting impact on illustration both in the United Kingdom and Europe as well as America.

The artists involved in the Arts and Crafts Movement attempted to counter the ever intruding Industrial Revolution (the first wave of which lasted roughly from 1750-1850) by bringing the values of beautiful and inventive craftsmanship back into the sphere of everyday life. It must be noted that around the turn of the century the boundaries between what would today be termed 'fine art' as opposed to 'crafts' and 'design' were far more fluid and in many cases non-operational, and many illustrators had lucrative painterly careers in addition to their design work. The Romanticism of the *Pre Raphaelite Brotherhood* combined with the intricate curvatures of the *Art Nouveaux* movement provided influential strands running through most illustrators work. The latter especially so for the Scottish illustrator Anne Anderson (1874-1930) as well as the Dutch artist Kay Nielson (1886-1957), who was also inspired by the stunning work of Japanese artists such as Hiroshige.

One of the main accomplishments of nineteenth century illustration lay in its ability to reach far wider numbers than the traditional 'high arts'. In 1892 the American critic William A. Coffin praised the new medium for popularising art; 'more has been done through the medium of illustrated literature… to make the masses of people realise that there is such a thing as art and that it is worth caring about'. Commercially, illustrated publications reached their zenith with the burgeoning 'Gift Book' industry which emerged in the first decade of the twentieth century. The first widely distributed gift book was published in 1905. It comprised of Washington Irving's short story *Rip Van Winkle* with the addition of 51 colour plates by a true master of illustration; Arthur Rackham. Rackham created each plate by first painstakingly drawing his subject in a sinuous pencil line before applying an ink layer – then he used layer upon layer of delicate watercolours to build up the romantic yet calmly ethereal results on which his reputation was constructed. Although Rackham is now one of the most recognisable names in illustration, his delicate palette owed no small debt to Kate Greenaway (1846-1901) – one of the first female illustrators whose pioneering and incredibly subtle use of the watercolour medium resulted in her election to the Royal Institute of Painters in Water Colours in 1889.

The year before Arthur Rackam's illustrations for *Rip Van Winkle* were published, a young and aspiring French artist by the name of Edmund Dulac (1882-1953) came to London and was to create a similarly impressive legacy. His timing could not have been more fortuitous. Several factors converged around the turn of the century which allowed illustrators and publishers alike a far greater freedom of creativity than previously imagined. The origination of the 'colour separation' practice meant that colour images, extremely faithful to the original artwork could be produced on a grand scale. Dulac possessed a rigorously painterly background (more so than his contemporaries) and was hence able to utilise the new technology so as to allow the colour itself to refine and define an object as opposed to the traditional pen and ink line. It has been estimated that in 1876 there was only one 'colour separation' firm in London, but by 1900 this number had rocketed to fifty. This improvement in printing quality also meant a reduction in labour, and coupled with the introduction of new presses and low-cost supplies of paper this meant that publishers could for the first time afford to pay high wages for highly talented artists.

Whilst still in the U.K, no survey of the *Golden Age of Illustration* would be complete without a mention of the Heath-Robinson brothers. Charles Robinson was renowned for his beautifully detached style, whether in pen and ink or sumptuous watercolours. Whilst William (the youngest) was to later garner immense fame for his carefully constructed yet tortuous machines operated by comical, intensely serious attendants. After World War One the Robinson brothers numbered among the few artists of the Golden Age who continued to regularly produce illustrated works. As we move towards the United States, one illustrator - Howard Pyle (1853-1911) stood head and shoulders above his contemporaries as the most distinguished illustrator of the age. From 1880 onwards Pyle illustrated over 100 volumes, yet it was not quantity which ensured his precedence over other American (and European) illustrators, but quality.

Pyle's sumptuous illustrations benefitted from a meticulous composition process livened with rich colour and deep recesses, providing a visual framework in which tales such as *Robin Hood* and *The Four Volumes of the Arthurian Cycle* could come to life. These are publications which remain continuous good sellers up till the present day. His flair and originality combined with a thoroughness of planning and execution were principles which he passed onto his many pupils at the *Drexel Institute of Arts and Sciences*. Two such pupils were Jessie Willcox Smith (1863-1935) who went on to illustrate books such as *The Water Babies* and *At the Back of North Wind* and perhaps most famously Maxfield Parrish (1870-1966) who became famed for luxurious colour (most remarkably demonstrated in his blue paintings) and imaginative designs; practices in no short measure gleaned from his tutor. As an indication of Parrish's popularity, in 1925 it was estimated that one fifth of American households possessed a Parrish reproduction.

As is evident from this brief introduction to the 'Golden Age of Illustration', it was a period of massive technological change and artistic ingenuity. The legacy of this enormously important epoch lives on in the present day – in the continuing popularity and respect afforded to illustrators, graphic and fine artists alike. This *Origins of Fairy Tales from Around the World* series will hopefully provide a fascinating insight into an era of intense historical and creative development, bringing both little known stories, and the art that has accompanied them, back to life.

Other titles in the 'Origins of Fairy Tales from Around the World' series...

CINDERELLA
AND OTHER GIRLS WHO
LOST THEIR SLIPPERS
ORIGINS OF FAIRY TALES
FROM AROUND THE WORLD

RUMPELSTILTSKIN
AND OTHER ANGRY IMPS WITH
RATHER UNUSUAL NAMES
ORIGINS OF FAIRY TALES
FROM AROUND THE WORLD

PUSS IN BOOTS
AND OTHER VERY CLEVER CATS
ORIGINS OF FAIRY TALES
FROM AROUND THE WORLD

SLEEPING BEAUTY
AND OTHER TALES OF
SLUMBERING PRINCESSES
ORIGINS OF FAIRY TALES
FROM AROUND THE WORLD

LITTLE RED RIDING HOOD
AND OTHER GIRLS WHO
GOT LOST IN THE WOODS
ORIGINS OF FAIRY TALES
FROM AROUND THE WORLD

RAPUNZEL
AND OTHER FAIR MAIDENS
IN VERY TALL TOWERS
ORIGINS OF FAIRY TALES
FROM AROUND THE WORLD

SNOW WHITE
AND OTHER EXAMPLES OF
JEALOUSY UNREWARDED
ORIGINS OF FAIRY TALES
FROM AROUND THE WORLD

BLUEBEARD
AND OTHER MYSTERIOUS MEN WITH
EVEN STRANGER FACIAL HAIR
ORIGINS OF FAIRY TALES
FROM AROUND THE WORLD

HANSEL AND GRETEL
AND OTHER SIBLINGS
FORSAKEN IN FORESTS
ORIGINS OF FAIRY TALES
FROM AROUND THE WORLD

Printed in Poland
by Amazon Fulfillment
Poland Sp. z o.o., Wrocław

53131279R00095